Pippa Roscoe lives in Norfolk near her family and makes daily promises to herself that *this* is the day she'll leave the computer to take a long walk in the countryside. She can't remember a time when she wasn't dreaming about handsome heroes and innocent heroines. Totally her mother's fault, of course—she gave Pippa her first romance to read at the age of seven! She is inconceivably happy that she gets to share those daydreams with you. Follow her on Twitter @PippaRoscoe.

RECLAIMED BY THE POWERFUL SHEIKH

PIPPA ROSCOE

MILLS & BOON

First Published in Great Britain 2019
by Mills & Boon, an imprint of HarperCollins*Publishers*
1 London Bridge Street, London, SE1 9GF

© 2019 Pippa Roscoe

ISBN: 978-0-263-08024-7

MIX
Paper from
responsible sources
FSC
www.fsc.org   FSC® C007454

This book is produced from independently certified FSC™ paper
to ensure responsible forest management.
For more information visit www.harpercollins.co.uk/green.

Printed and bound in Great Britain
by CPI Group (UK) Ltd, Croydon, CR0 4YY

PROLOGUE

MASON MCAULTY COULDN'T tell if she was breathing.

It was highly likely, an automatic physical directive obeyed by her body through necessity, but often during a race she didn't have the time to remind herself to do it. But then, often during a race she didn't have unwanted thoughts intruding on her mind. Usually her mind was like a cool stream running quick and clear. Not this time. Mason should be focused on the horse beneath her, not the man from her past—the man in her present—the man she wanted to run from. Danyl.

She stopped short the shiver of ache that vibrated within her chest from thoughts of what might have been before it could take hold. Before it could synchronise with the rhythm of the pounding of horses' hooves and overwhelm her. She shoved the thought away and focused on the invisible line halfway round the racetrack, beyond a corner that was coming up. Very quickly.

The burn in her thighs, holding her just above Veranchetti's spine, felt good. Felt right. Sound in her ears was nothing but an unending roar. Her knees, absorbing the undulations of the horse beneath her. Hooves thundering in place of a heartbeat. For her. For Veranchetti. They were perfectly in time with each other.

This.

This was what sent adrenaline coursing through her veins. It wasn't like flying, it wasn't effortless, it wasn't easy. It took fierce determination, muscle, control, understanding and intuition to harness the power of such a horse, to be able to direct that power, to be able to meet that power and do incredible things together.

Mason could have been riding for hours, years even, but it had only been seconds. Perhaps only as long as a minute. But it was the last eighteen months that condensed into this moment. Nothing else mattered, but everything mattered. She had to win this race. For her father. For herself. For everything that she'd been through and everything that she would go through.

With ruthless focus, Mason blocked out the thoughts, blocked out the sight of the horse in front of her, the one beside her and the many behind her. She blinkered her vision, just like Veranchetti, as they came to the last corner on the flat race.

Anticipation rose within her like lightening glass, twisting and twining inside her, solidifying into a tangible thing. This was the moment that Veranchetti came into his own. As if he too blocked everything out until the very last second.

This was the moment when she allowed herself a small smile. The moment Veranchetti threw himself into the race, as if everything before had just been to get them to this point. She felt it in him, the moment he found that inconceivable burst of strength, the moment

that he surged ahead, the moment he surprised everyone but her.

The moment when there was only a breath between
victory and failure. Between past and present, present
and future.

Just one moment…one breath.

CHAPTER ONE

December, present day

DANYL NEJEM AL ARAIN needed to breathe. Needed to focus on what one of his best friends and co-owners of the Winners' Circle Syndicate was saying. But he couldn't. His mind was being torn in a million different directions, all pointing to the royal palace's gala in a week's time. The gala that would be the final undoing of his sanity.

'Antonio, I—'

'Have to go, yeah, I got it. Things to do, countries to run... Listen, don't worry. John and Veranchetti are on their way.'

'On their way to where?' Danyl asked, the suspicion sneaking through his usually quick mind deeply unsettling.

'To Ter'harn.'

'What?'

'As per your mother's request. As they were already set to come to you for the New Year's Day meet, she asked that they arrive a few weeks early so that they could be part of the celebrations.'

'This gala is getting completely out of hand.'

'Not as much as my soon-to-be mother-in-law's wedding plans. Fifty doves. The woman wants to release
fifty doves as we leave the church. Never has Las Vegas
looked so appealing!'

'Las Vegas?' Danyl struggled to keep track of the
words pouring from Antonio's mouth.

'Are you even listening to me?' Impatience bit into
the earpiece of the phone.

'Las Vegas. If you really want to move the wedding
there, count me in,' Danyl said, forcing an energy he
didn't feel into the promise.

'Appreciated. Look, the point of the call… I need to
know who your plus one will be for the wedding. So,
who do you have up next to audition for the role as your
future and perfect Queen? I have to admit, from what
Dimitri said about Birgetta—'

'I'll let you know, when *I* know,' Danyl bit back.

'It's just that, given the recent press attention from
McAulty's win, we're having to get extra security in
place.'

'Got it. Look, I'll get back to you on the plus one. And
I'll see you and Emma in a week for the gala.'

Danyl hung up on whatever response Antonio would
have given, knowing that his friend would forgive him.

Things to do, countries to run…

He slipped his phone into his pocket, rather than hurling it across the room as he wanted. What on earth was
his mother thinking, bringing their racing syndicate's
trainer John and their prize thoroughbred Veranchetti to
the gala? Not only that, but also to go behind his back and
speak directly to Dimitri and Antonio? She was clearly
up to something and he had to put a stop to it. Now. The
more she added to the line-up of entertainment, the more

risk there was that something would go wrong, that it wouldn't be perfect. And the gala *had* to be perfect.

He backed the chair away from the solid wooden desk piled high with paperwork and yellow legal notepads full of his tightly scrawled handwriting, so different from the sleek glass design and state-of-the-art technology of his office in central Aram, capital of Ter'harn. He missed the smooth efficiency and calm simplicity of his professional setting, gently cursing his mother for the melodrama that had brought him reluctantly back to the royal palace.

Entering the hallway sent a couple of house staff scattering and drew his personal bodyguard along in his wake. His parents would be in the dining room at this hour, Danyl was sure of it. Marching along the hallways with brusque determination, he failed to take in the centuries of elaborate decoration lining the walls, the fine tiled details on the flooring, soft earthy tones contrasting with bright whites, blues and greens, yet his shoulders still felt the burden of the palace. If he twitched them in reflex, he didn't realise it.

Ter'harn was an oil-rich country, perfectly placed for both the desert climate and the almost Mediterranean temperature of the mountainous coastline that gave way to the Arabian Sea. It was a heady mix of cultures and influences, everything from the remains of the Ottoman Empire to modern Africa and Arabic nations, brought together within Ter'harn's borders. Of the country's three palaces, this was by far the grandest. It had withstood five centuries, three invasions and one attempted coup. Every corner, hallway, room and garden proudly displayed the fingerprints of those who had come before. Whilst other countries had shifted allegiances, royals and rulers, Ter'harn was one of the few kingdoms that had stayed immovable. His family one of the last to remain unseated. It was all resting on his shoulders. And to ensure that their legacy continued, he needed to find a queen to provide an heir. A thought that twisted and turned in Danyl's stomach.

Travelling at such a speed didn't give the house staff enough time to announce his presence at the dining-room doorway, a mistake he realised only too late.

His father and mother were by the window in what could only be described as a *clinch*. His father's hands clutching his mother's...

Danyl spun on his heel, facing the wall as if *he* had been caught out rather than his parents. He wasn't a prude. But they were his parents!

He cleared his throat, heard a somewhat flustered response and a shifting of movement, counted to ten, and then an extra five for good measure, before turning back to find them facing him, neither a hair out of place nor a shred of embarrassment visible.

'Did you really need to bring Veranchetti halfway round the world for a party? Don't you think it a little ostentatious to parade a horse from my syndicate in front of all your guests?'

'Darling, we're fine, thank you for asking. It is good to see you too,' his mother mocked. She often complained that he only had one speed: ruthless efficiency. 'We're royal, Danyl. People are going to think that anything we do is ostentatious. We might as well have a little fun and play up to it, no? You used to love playing up to it,' she said, unable to hide the hint of censure that often came with such a declaration. A silent reminder that he used to have fun. Once. 'Besides, I simply spoke to the boys—'

'They are not boys, Mother.'

'I have known them since you were all at university together. You were boys then, and you'll always be boys to me.'

'You went behind my back.'

'Oh, Danyl, don't be so dramatic.' Her exasperation was undermined by an overly emphatic and somewhat disappointed sigh. 'Veranchetti was already due to come to Ter'harn and you know that. I simply asked if they would be able to move up the date of their arrival for the New Year's Day race to coincide with the gala, which is—in part—a celebration of your achievements.'

'I would hardly call it *my* achievement, Mother,' Danyl replied.

'Ah, yes. The delightful Mason McAulty. She has yet to respond to our invitation.'

'You invited Mason?' If his mother noticed the ice-cool tone his voice had contained, she didn't show it.

'Yes, what a wonderful feat, winning all the three races in the Hanley Cup. Quite extraordinary. For a woman.'

Elizabeth Al Arain's words settled into a buzzing sound between Danyl's ears. Just Mason McAulty's name was enough to short-circuit his perfectly ordered mind. Images of thick, dark brown hair curling over a sun-kissed shoulder haunted his mind, the echo of a laugh from ten years before, the slight smell of leather and hay...odd scents of feminine silk-soft skin. His mind reared back in self-defence and Danyl sought anger, fury, anything to cover over the moment of mental weakness her name had brought.

Mason McAulty.

He didn't want her here. Not in Ter'harn, not in the palace. He hadn't even wanted her to ride in the Hanley

Cup for their syndicate the Winners' Circle, but Dimitri Kyriakou and Antonio Arcuri had been quite taken with the idea. Two against one. Although, in all likelihood, if Danyl had refused they would have accepted his decision without question. But the moment she had approached them in the exclusive private members' club in London…frankly he'd been shocked. Shocked enough to utter a few barbed comments Mason had refused to rise to. He'd tried to send her away, but the stubborn woman had refused. And most of all, that had been what had impressed the Winners' Circle. That and the sheer audacity of what she'd suggested. Who could have imagined that she would deliver on her promise?

'Well, I want her here,' his mother pressed on. 'You know how much I love horse racing. Where do you think you got the bug from?'

'My investment in horses is not a "bug".'

'Danyl Nejem Al Arain, do not take that tone with me. What Mason McAulty has achieved is nothing short of miraculous. Coming first in each of the three legs of the Hanley Cup with horses from one syndicate—*your* syndicate—hasn't been achieved in over thirty years. You know that, I know that, and I want to celebrate the success of such an incredible female jockey. I always thought that had I not been an actress—'

'You would have liked to be a jockey, yes, I know. But you were too tall, Mother.'

Her response was a delicate sniff. 'It didn't stop me from being an excellent rider though. I want to meet this young woman, Danyl, and I want you to do whatever it takes to make it happen. Go to Australia in person, if you have to. Either way, consider it an early Christmas present.'

'What are you really getting out of this, Mother?' he asked, feeling his own eyes narrow in suspicion. But of what, he couldn't quite place, or he didn't want to.

'Oh, darling, it will be the best party we've had here for years. With relationships on the borders doing so well, thanks to all your hard work, your father and I are thinking of stepping back further to allow you the room to take the throne.'

Danyl cast a look to his father, silently watching the conversation as if intuiting undercurrents that Danyl was missing.

'But tradition dictates that you wait until I am married,' he said, fury giving way to frustration as a series of efficiently arranged dates with poised princesses and highly capable CEOs filtered through the last few months of his memory. Anything to prevent the full impact of his mother's words from raining down upon him. That he was finally going to ascend to the throne. That he would finally inherit the weight of responsibility for hundreds of centuries of culture and nearly three million people.

'Well, as you are failing so spectacularly to produce such a fiancée,' she said, gently mocking him, 'we can't wait for ever, can we? We're not getting any younger, and it's about time that I had my husband to myself for a change. Either way, that's what I want. Mason at the party. And I want you to do whatever it takes to make that happen.'

The morning heat was already fierce and Mason was conscious of time running out. She needed to get a move on if she was to get to the outer fencing of their Australian farmland. She hitched up the saddle strap one hole tighter, threading it back through the buckle as Fool's

Fate shifted on his hooves. She gave the horse's flank a reassuring pat and turned to find her father standing behind the saddlebags in the stable's courtyard.

He looked as if he had aged ten years, rather than the eighteen months she'd been away. The grey at his temples now firmly white. The hollows beneath his eyes a darker shade of blue. She toned down the flare of frustration, the painful ache of sadness, knowing Fool's Fate would pick up on her feelings if she vented them. Her father picked up one of the bags and held it out to her. She took it from him, turned back to the horse, strapping it to the saddle, and took the moment she needed.

Beyond the stables, the rolling emerald-coloured fields stretched out towards the mountains in the distance. Mountains that had always brought her a sense of peace, yet now seemed to loom as some kind of dark prophecy. Taking a deep breath, she felt the warm air fill her lungs, heavy and hot.

Joe McAulty had something on his mind. Not that he'd open his mouth to speak until he was ready. There was no rushing the man, never had been and never would be. So she just carried on packing the saddle bags until he said his piece.

Tent, phone, food, she mentally ticked off, coffee…

'I didn't think he'd call it in so soon.'

'Pops, it can't be helped.' It was the same response she'd made when he'd first told her about the debt collection.

'But after everything you did, the purses you won from the Hanley Cup…'

'Pops, Mick died.' She threw the words over her shoulder, shrugging off the swell of grief she felt for the neighbour who'd seemed an old coot even when she was a child. But her dad was a plain speaker, and emotions were an unknown language over which he stuttered and stumbled. 'Who could have known that his son would call in the debt so soon? And yeah, if he hadn't, the money from the wins might have kept us going for a couple of years, but something else might have come up.'

She finally allowed herself to turn around. Her father was kicking the dirt floor, keeping his focus on the spray of dust caught in the sun's early rays.

'The farm isn't lost yet, Pops.' Mason knew he felt responsible, but she couldn't blame him. Not at all. 'Our work, the work we do with the kids here, it's as important to me as it is to you. And it's expensive. Keeping all the horses, the counsellors, the physios, the staff… Mick's son calling in the loan, it's just something we have to deal with.' Another something, she said to herself, to add to the many others. 'Joe,' she said, calling him by the same name all the other farmhands and staff used, finally getting his attention. 'I'm not going to let this go without a fight. Especially to that trumped-up wannabe ranch owner.'

A sad smile pulled at the corner of his mouth. Defiance was something that ran through them both in spades. She turned back to the horse behind her, faking the need to check the bags one more time. 'Perhaps I can find another syndicate to race for. There'll be plenty of options after the Hanley Cup.'

'I wouldn't ask you to do that.' Her father's voice had lowered, full of the same gravel and grit he'd just kicked up off the floor.

'It wasn't that bad, Dad,' she said, unable to turn to face him. He'd know. He'd raised her singlehandedly from the age of two. There wasn't a secret she could keep, a lie she could tell, without him knowing. Racing again… No, it hadn't been as bad as she'd thought. Riding Veranchetti had made her feel…alive. Complete in a way she hadn't felt for years. But it had been hard. Had thrown up a lot of feelings. Ones that she needed to sort through. Which was why she had decided to go and fix the outposts herself.

Yes, riding had been tough, but Danyl? No. Her feelings about him hadn't been hard to discern at all. She needed to stay away from him at all costs.

Mason swept up the tendrils of her long, dark hair into a band, allowing the cool breeze to nip at her hot neck, and watched the sun set between the giant clefts of the mountains bordering the Hunter River Valley, breathing in the first calm lungful of air she'd tasted in almost eighteen months. The ride out here had been incredible, the familiar dips and rises of the stunning horse farm she'd been lucky enough to grow up on as familiar as the wooden knots on the farmstead's dining-room table.

Whenever she came out here, whenever she saw the sweeping stretches of the green valley, bordered by mountains that seemed like immoveable watchtowers guarding the land, she found herself wondering how her mother could have left. Her father had tried to explain over the years, the yearning for something *more* that her mother had felt. And perhaps, if Mason was honest with herself, she had felt a thread of that too when she'd gone to America to train as a jockey ten years ago. But home and wanting wasn't at the *end* of a rainbow. It was at the start of it. She'd learned that lesson hard. Mason wouldn't regret leaving, but she'd not be doing it again.

She brought the steaming hot mug to her lips and inhaled the scent of roasted coffee beans, wet earth and the wood near by. If she discerned the aroma of sweat, hay, manure, grief and something male she refused to acknowledge it—just her memory playing tricks again.

Before her, the night sky crept over the valley's emerald patchwork quilt and it wouldn't take long for it to reach behind her and the farm that she had tried so very hard to save. The money from the purses of the three races she'd won for the Winners' Circle should have been enough. She stamped down the little voice in her heart that pleaded to know why it wasn't. She had never been one for self-pity, and if she had? She would have been done for, long before now.

She'd have spoken to Mick's son if she didn't already know he was a bottom feeder, wanting to turn the farm next to theirs into prime real estate, wanting to sell off land that had been in his family for nearly seven generations to the highest bidder. Money. Why did it always come down to money?

What she and her father did on their farm, the way they helped troubled kids—kids with learning difficulties, kids that just needed something positive in their lives—interact with horses, learn to ride, to care for another living thing and be cared for in return…there was no price to put on that. When Pops had been forced to stay at the farm, to give up his training career to raise her after her mother had left, he'd seen a way to carry on what he loved most. His love for the horses was now spread through hundreds of children, teenagers and young adults. It might not have been a fix-all, it might not have helped every child that passed through the farm, but it had helped enough. The sheer delight at seeing a child, unable to look anyone in the eye, finally come out of themselves, transform into something brighter, the first smile, laugh, in what looked like years for some of them... That was worth it all.

But in order to continue they needed to expand. They needed more room for the counsellors, staff and children. They weren't operating at a loss as such, but without increasing the scope of the business they wouldn't survive either. And now with the loan? The purse money would go to that, and they were back at square one. Everything she'd done in the last eighteen months, wiped clean.

Coffee hit her stomach hard as Mason considered riding in another race. The last three had been physically and mentally challenging. Though reluctant to admit it, ten years made a difference to a body and the training had been intense. The first thing her dad had done when she'd returned to the farm after the race series was force-feed her enough food to feed an army. She hadn't lost weight as much as body fat, all of it turning to enough muscle to harness the power of the two incredible horses she'd had for the Hanley Cup. Eighteen months of six day a weeks, morning and afternoon training, one meal days.

She might have left racing after what had happened ten years ago, but her body hadn't forgotten, and there hadn't been a day in between that she hadn't been on a horse. Her father had said she'd been born to it, and the pride at the time...the pride before had been enough to make her want to fulfil that childhood dream of being Australia's best jockey. Not best *female* jockey. Just best jockey.

And for a few moments, riding Veranchetti and Devil's Advocate, she'd felt that need unfurl within her, the knowledge that she could make it happen, she could still have that childish dream and turn it into reality...it had been seductive, a whisper of what could be.

But to race again, for a different syndicate, on different horses? No. She knew that wasn't an option. Neither was going back to the Winners' Circle.

There had been plenty of journos just waiting to get her story, and the money they were offering for interviews and photoshoots would be worth considering if it hadn't been those very same people who had destroyed her career first time round. The coffee turned bitter on her tongue, and she knew that even as a last resort she couldn't do it. She had learnt enough about herself to respect the person she had become, and to honour that by being truthful and faithful and kind to herself. It might have taken these last ten years, but she wouldn't sell herself out to the highest bidder.

The sun had now firmly set behind the mountains, stars beginning to wink out of the night sky. Fool's Fate pricked his ears and snickered, pawing at the ground and shifting his head against the rope tied to a tree behind her.

Mason frowned, as the sounds of crunched twigs and leaves met her ears. It wouldn't be Pops, not knowing that she wanted to be alone. And the farmhands were out in town tonight, settled in at the pub. It couldn't be anyone from Mick's farm, the border between their land too far away from her camp. That just left poachers. She threw her coffee over the embers of the fire, sending a hiss out into the air, and reached for her shotgun.

Danyl cursed into the dark as the glimmer of light he'd seen from a fire disappeared. It had been a beacon and now he could only smell burnt coffee and damp ash. Perhaps he should have listened to Joe McAulty. He'd left his horse tied up a little way back because he hadn't wanted to scare her. He felt twigs crunch and crack under his feet, the sound echoing like gunfire in the silence of the night. Ignoring the feeling in his gut, the one that poked at him as if to say that perhaps he shouldn't have left his men back at the farm, he pressed on. He couldn't have had this conversation in front of an audience. His men hadn't been happy about it, but they'd done as he'd commanded.

He came out from underneath the wooded area, and for a moment the beauty of the sight stopped him. The night scene before him stole his breath; it almost matched the awe he felt when he looked out at the Ter'harn desert. That's why, he told himself later, it took a moment to realise the camp that he'd overlooked was empty. The moon passed behind a cloud, casting the still smoking fire and the small tent in shadow.

He cursed again, exhausted and frustrated. Where the hell was she? No longer disguising his footfalls, he stomped into the clearing. Given the flight, the particularly painful meeting with Ter'harn's Prime Minister, and the even more barbed conversation with Joe McAulty, Danyl had just about had enough.

He scanned the site again, looking for signs of where she might be. He'd followed Joe's instructions, and clearly found where she had set up, but—

The sound of the chamber being pulled back on a pump-action shotgun stopped his thoughts in their tracks. Logic did nothing to slow the sudden jolt of adrenaline coursing through his veins. Logically he knew it was Mason, logically he knew that she wouldn't shoot him. But still…

'You shouldn't have come here,' he heard a voice from behind him say.

CHAPTER TWO

December, ten years ago

'I SHOULDN'T HAVE come here,' Mason said, pulling at the short hemline of the dress Francesca had somehow talked her into wearing.

'It's New Year's Eve, Mase! It's time you let your hair down instead of being all train, train, train, diet, exercise, no alcohol, no fun,' her friend replied in the rapid-fire American accent Mason was only just about getting used to.

'I look ludicrous.'

'Are you insane? You look fab-u-lous!' Francesca replied, hanging on to every syllable of the word.

'How are you supposed to walk in these instruments of torture?'

'Wash your mouth out—those are Louboutins,' she said, this time slicing the brand into almost three separate words.

'Then perhaps he should have stuck with boots,' Mason muttered under her breath.

'What?'

'Never mind.'

'Listen, girly, I know you only got off the boat four months ago—'

'It was a plane.'

'And America isn't Australia, and New York isn't the hick town in whatever part of New South Wales you're from, but it's time to acclimatise to these surroundings.'

Mason bridled at the comment, her shoulders squaring at the slight against her home, softening only when she caught sight of Francesca's tongue, literally pressed against the inside of her cheek.

But, stealing another glance at the surroundings, Mason felt as if this was a glimpse into a world in which she did not belong. That perhaps if she stared too long, or stayed too long, she might lose herself.

When the bus from the training stables had dropped them off outside one of New York's most renowned hotels, the Langsford, she had looked up at the huge, sweeping circular driveway, the gilded graphics on the Roman-style pillars that fronted the building, and thought... *They're not going to let me in here.*

Between with the heels Francesca had forced her into and the black and white marble foyer, she'd nearly broken her ankle as she'd walked towards the biggest spiral staircase she'd ever seen. And even Francesca had let out a low whistle when she'd seen the 'reception room' hired for the night's event, arranged by America's richest horse owners.

Smooth, sleek lines of chrome and black dropped away at the floor-to-ceiling windows looking out over Washington Square Park and the surrounding area. Purple NYU flags hung from buildings and a few brave souls were risking hypothermia out in the snow-covered streets, revelling or hurrying towards whatever party or group they were out to join before midnight.

A smartly dressed waiter passed with a tray of cham-

pagne flutes, a small piece of strawberry the only adorn-
ment to the alcohol. Francesca grabbed two glasses,
thrust one into her hands so quickly she nearly dropped
it, and Mason watched, shocked, as Francesca took a
third before allowing the waiter to move on.

Francesca consumed the entire contents of the first
glass in one mouthful before placing it on a side table,
and flashed Mason a beaming grin before returning to
sip from the second. Her eyes locked on to something
over Mason's shoulder, a whispered excuse trailing behind in the wake of a speedy departure. Mason turned to
find Harry, their trainer, making his way towards them…
or, well, Mason at least.

'You doing okay?'

'I'm…acclimatising,' she said and smiled at her father's old friend, before taking a sip of champagne. It
was expensive, but not very nice.

'You're doing better than Joe would have.'

'No.' She smiled ruefully, thinking of how he might
have behaved amongst these people. 'Pops wouldn't have
acclimatised to this very well.'

Harry grinned. He was a large man, who smiled
deeply, laughed heartily and trained his jockeys to within
an inch of their lives. 'This is an opportunity for you to
meet some of the horse-racing syndicates that may take
you on in the future.'

Confusion marred Mason's brow. 'I thought you were
happy with O'Conner.'

'I am, and I'm looking forward to the first race of
the season, but that doesn't mean I, or you, will be riding and training for him for the rest of our careers. You
never know, you could be riding for one of the people in
this room within the year.'

Mason turned to scan the room with different eyes. This time she saw people forging connections, not just small talk, not just flirting, but making investments in their future. As her eyes traversed the room, they caught on one particular figure at the edge of the crowd, his elbow leaning against the bar, at least a head taller than those around him.

Power. Raw and untamed.

It was the first thought she had, the moment her eyes rested on him. Although his body cut a lazy figure, seeming almost bored in the way his head leant to one side, there was something leashed about him. Tension thrummed through his body, vibrating at a pitch she was surprised those about him couldn't feel. *She* could. All the way from the other side of the room.

Dark, thick hair fell in slight waves around a face that wouldn't have looked out of place on a marble statue of perfect male beauty. Skin smooth over his brow, deeply tanned, the colour of the darkest whisky and just as tempting. High cheekbones perfectly captured her gaze, and for a moment she just stared. A trace of stubble on his firm jaw made the palms of her hands tingle, made her want to reach out and feel the texture beneath her skin, made her want to hear the sound of it rasp against her.

She cursed herself for the foolish thought, but couldn't pull her gaze away. He seemed to be listening to a group of men, but something told her that he wasn't really paying attention. It was his eyes. They weren't focused on the man speaking, but somewhere over the man's shoulder. Then he turned his head slowly, not scanning the room, not aimlessly wandering, but, deliberate, clear, and directed straight at her. His eyes caught hold of her gaze, and refused to let it go.

The burn of a blush against her cheeks was instantaneous. She dropped her eyes, shocked by the spark of electricity that had hissed and snapped its way up her spine, across her skin and into her chest. She chanced a glance back towards the man who had incited such an extreme reaction, only to feel it all over again as her eyes joined his once more.

A gasp?

Had she really gasped?

She turned to Harry in an attempt to sever the connection, but Harry was gone and she was standing alone. Now the blush was one of pure embarrassment. She must look to him exactly what she was—a country bumpkin, or 'hick', as Francesca had remarked earlier.

That was when she heard a uniquely feminine laugh from somewhere near to the man who had run a lightning streak through her. Of course. When she looked back, she saw that Francesca had joined the circle of awe around the figure whose eyes were no longer on Mason, but on her beautiful, laughing friend.

'Hey.' A familiar voice called for Mason's attention.

Scott was making his way towards her on slightly unsteady feet. How had he managed to drink so much already? 'I hate these things,' he complained.

Mason let out a huff of air, thankful for the distraction offered by the trainee jockey from whatever had just happened. No, she wasn't naïve enough not to know what it was, but it was certainly the first time she'd felt anything like what she'd read in the romance books that were the only thing her mother had left behind.

'Not really my thing either,' she said, turning the half-drunk glass of champagne around in her hands. She made a face at the thought of the alcohol, probably warm now, and put it on the table next to Francesca's discarded, *empty,* glass.

'Wanna get out of here?'

'The bus isn't coming for at least another three and a half hours, Scott.'

'Fresh air. There's a balcony that wraps around the back of the building.'

Resisting the pull of one last glance at the man, re- luctant to feel that punishing spark once more, she took the arm that Scott had offered and let him lead her from the room.

The American girl's laugh was grating on what little nerves Danyl had left. The whole evening had been a bust. He was beginning to think that perhaps he should have returned to Ter'harn, to his parents... Until he'd caught sight of the little brunette over in the corner. He'd felt her gaze on him across the room. It was as if a flame had licked across his cheek. In the three and a half years he'd been in New York for his degree and masters in busi- ness and international relations, he'd not felt anything like it. But he knew what it meant. And it usually came with a giant neon sign saying *STAY AWAY* in capital letters.

But, despite the warning, he hadn't been able to break the connection. She was petite, tiny even, in comparison to his near six feet and four inches, but every single inch of her spoke of strength. Her skin, sun-kissed and lightly tanned, even in the depths of this New York winter had warmed him all over. And his fingers itched to run and play in the sweeping curls of her long hair the colour of burnt sugar. Sweet, the taste on his tongue imaginary and expectant, but as sure as if he'd just eaten a single caramel.

Within one distracted moment, she'd disappeared and he wondered if it was for the best. Danyl looked at his watch. Perhaps he should head back to the embassy. Surely there would be more life in their end-of-year party than this. A morgue would beat this. At first, the thought of having all of America's best racing syndicates in one room sounded fantastic. A chance to research what had only been a briefly mentioned idea by Antonio a couple of months ago but, taken up by Danyl and Dimitri, was fast becoming a deeply tempting business prospect—to create a world-renowned horse-racing syndicate of their own. They'd toyed with the name for a while, but they kept coming back around to the Winners' Circle. Only they couldn't decide where to put the apostrophe.

They should have been here with him. The two students he'd met nearly four years ago at the beginning of their studies had soon become the brothers he'd never had. Having been thrust into the American lifestyle of university, they had been drawn together by the determination to succeed not only in their studies, but also in their pleasures. And the bond of friendship born from similar interests had become something more...vital. Never before had Danyl had such close friendships, the palace being a lonely place for an only child. An only *royal* child.

This evening was supposed to have been *it*! Been *amazing*. It was the last New Year's Eve he would spend in New York before he went back to Ter'harn and the life of duty that awaited him. And he'd wanted to make it count, wanted it to be the last, greatest chance to let loose, to be...free. But Antonio had been forced to visit his parents and sister, and Dimitri was rescuing his half-brother from some scandal back in Greece.

So here he was, alone at the Langsford, where it seemed he couldn't escape his royal reputation and the conversation had turned to him instead of horses and racing. For a moment, he thought he might have found something else in the eyes of a dark-haired, dark-eyed beauty, but she had disappeared and instead some brash American was making a pass at him. In front of everyone.

She laughed again and that was it.

Forgoing the usual diplomatic politeness that felt as if it had been forced, rather than bred, into him, he walked out of the human circle, leaving one of the men midsentence. They'd forgive him. He was royalty after all.

Heading for the exit, he spied the evening's patrons and knew that he would be waylaid if they saw him. He veered off to a glass doorway leading to the balcony, where, if he was lucky, there might just be a door back in at the other end of it. He ducked out onto the large wraparound balcony and the sting of the frigid wintry air bit at him, but even that was nothing compared to the shock he'd felt when he'd locked eyes with that girl. It was a shame to leave without seeing what that could have led to, but safer. Yes, definitely safer.

The sounds of hushed angry voices were thrown against him by the whipping wind. He frowned, looking out into the shadows to see two figures just before the bend in the building. A man and...*that* woman. Before his body could react, he saw her pull her hand away from the man's clutches, only to be pinned against the brick wall behind her.

'Get off me, Scott.'

'Don't give me that, Mase...' The man's slurred voice was muffled by the way his head was buried in her neck.

'You're making a fool of yourself. Just stop it.' The woman's words were firm rather than angry as she tried to push him away.

'Oh, come on, Mason, you've been making eyes at me for nearly three months now.'

'I've done nothing of the sort, Scott. I'm going back inside.'

'No, you're not.' The man reached out to grab her arm again in the time that it took Danyl to cover the distance between them.

'Get off me!'

'The lady told you to stop.' Danyl's loud voice was toned with barely leashed control. He hated men like that. Hated when a man couldn't take the word no.

'Go away. This is none of your business.'

Danyl peered at the brunette in the darkness. There was nothing about her that suggested she was faking her distress. Her eyes were large, deep brown pools marred by frustration and even a little fear. Her body was held tight, retreating on itself as if to reduce the physical contact between her and this guy as much as possible.

The man spun round to face Danyl, squaring up to him with arrogance and inebriation.

'If anyone's leaving, it's—'

Danyl had seen the move coming from a mile away, the man's whole body thrown into a wide, arcing punch that held more bravado than power. It really took very little effort for Danyl to block the man's punch with his forearm and thrust up his free hand into the man's nose.

A rather unpleasant crunching sound cut into the night, seemingly worse for the woman's gasp of shock and the subsequent howl let out by the man now bent double, clutching his nose.

The man scuttled over to the door to the balcony, casting a furious glance at Danyl and the woman whose name he still didn't know, before re-entering the building, dropping curses like litter in his wake.

Danyl looked back at the woman who had stepped away from the wall, a delicate shiver running across her skin. Her eyes, almost as dark as the night, stared up at him, any trace of fear vanished, and instead he was surprised to find anger.

'Are you—?'

'What the hell did you do that for?' she demanded, husky Australian accents heavy on her words.

'What?'

'I had it under control,' she muttered under her breath, pushing past Danyl. He tried to ignore the spark her touch brought, and focus on the reaction he hadn't expected.

'Like hell you did,' he replied, spinning around to face her. 'That guy was—'

'Drunk and harmless. I could have handled him myself,' she dismissed.

'Of course you could have. Look at you. You can't be taller than five feet and two inches!'

'Size doesn't matter,' she responded indignantly.

He narrowed his gaze, desperately fighting back the instinctive retort to the contrary. But it seemed she had read his thoughts as clearly as if he'd said them.

'Really?' she demanded, and the scorn in her voice was a little too much for Danyl to bear. Perhaps he should have just stayed out of it. Facing the event's patrons would have been better than this.

She huffed out an impressively delicate puff of air and disappeared through the door to the reception.

* * *

Mason shook out her hands, a slight trembling the only outward sign of what had happened on the balcony she would allow herself to show. What had Scott been thinking? He had taken her completely by surprise, never having shown any interest in her other than that of a friend. Until now. And contrary to what that stranger had thought, she *did* have it under control. If she could wrangle an unstable stock horse, she could handle Scott. She willed the adrenaline coursing through her veins from her fight—rather than flight—reaction to leave her body, more angry than scared that she had found herself in that situation. No. That Scott had put her in that situation. She hadn't seen or heard anything about Scott that indicated he was...*like that*, and Mason *could* have handled it herself. But someone else might not. So, she'd be speaking to Harry about it in the morning.

What she hadn't been able to handle was her reaction to the man who had driven her out to the balcony in the first place. The man who had broken Scott's nose. She had tried to avoid his gaze and the intense, searing heat she felt every time they locked eyes. As the shivers from just the memory of it wracked her body, she told herself it was from the cold, but knew she was made of sterner stuff than that. The thrill of just being near him was incredible, and she'd only ever felt such a thing galloping down the gentle slopes of her father's horse farm back in New South Wales.

As she stood in the small hallway that either led back to the reception, or to the bank of lifts that might take her away from the Langsford, the muffled sound of the party reached her ears and she knew she didn't want to go back in there. She quickly retrieved her long,

thick coat from the cloakroom, changed out of the painfully high heels into warmer and much more comfortable black boots and slipped into the lift before anyone
could see her leave.

As Mason descended nearly thirty flights, she calculated how long she'd have until the bus came back to
pick them up. Two, maybe three hours. She looked at
herself in the gold-tinted mirrored panels, and instead
saw two hazel eyes in a chiselled marble image of male
perfection staring at her as if he knew something about
her *she* didn't know.

'I had it under control,' she whispered angrily to the
image of a man she feared she might never forget.

The doors to the lift opened and she strode across the
black and white chessboard foyer, her eyes cast down as
she held a stern conversation with herself. She'd definitely had it under control, she assured herself as she
pushed, too heavily, on the spinning circular doorway,
the resulting force shoving her out onto the pavement
beyond and straight into the back of...

Oof.

The air was knocked from her lungs the moment her
chest met a deliciously muscled back, even if it was a bit
painful. She reached out a hand to steady herself, only
to find that her fingers had wrapped around a forearm,
also disturbingly muscular.

'I'm so—'

Her apology was cut short as the stranger from the
balcony turned, pushing her off balance, and she would
have fallen if he hadn't pulled back the arm she was still
clinging to. Instead, she found herself chest to chest with
her apparent rescuer.

'We must stop—'

'Don't finish that cliché,' she warned.

'Are you always this angry?' he asked, the half-laughing, half-genuine curiosity dancing in his eyes.

'No, I'm just…' She shook her head to loosen the thoughts that were churned up by the very sight of him. 'Usually more coherent,' she added ruefully, an answering smile pulling at her lips.

She stepped back, away from the heat of him, the smell…something she wanted to take a little longer to discern. If she'd thought there was power in the man from across the room, being this close, being held by him, was overwhelming. Casting a glance upwards, she could see golden flecks in his impossibly dark eyes, flecks that sparkled with mischief. His lips, curved into an almost irresistible smile, were full and indiscreetly sensual, and Mason found herself responding in a way that was wholly unexpected and inappropriate.

She turned away from the sheer magnetism of the man and looked up and down the street, surprised to find it so quiet. Everyone must either be at their own party, or in Times Square, she mused as breath streamed like smoke into the night air about them.

This was silly. She had to get over him. Over *herself*, more like.

'Thank you,' she said, the words white on the air in front of them, neither, it seemed, willing to look at the other. 'For…' She used a hand to gesture up and behind her back towards the balcony.

From the corner of her eye, she saw his powerful shoulder shrug, and felt rather than watched his lips curve into an ironic smile. 'You had it under control.' A heartbeat later, 'You're leaving?' his accented voice asked. She couldn't place it. Somewhere from the Arab states, clearly. But not one she'd encountered at her father's horse farm before.

She frowned at his question. 'No,' she said, once more looking up and down the strangely quiet street. She offered her own shrugged shoulder. 'The bus coming to take us back to our accommodation isn't arriving until one a.m.'

'Our accommodation,' he mused. 'Our being you and…'

'The other trainee jockeys,' she said, deliberately ignoring his leading question.

'One of whom would be…'

'Scott. Yes. He is one of the other trainee jockeys.'

'And you don't want to go back to the party.' It was a statement and a warning, all in one.

Mason pursed her lips into a pout and shook her head, still looking out into the street before her, rather than see—or feel—his eyes on her.

'I'm hungry,' he announced in a way that seemed to involve her somehow. 'With absolutely no ulterior motive, would you like to go and get some food?'

She willed him silently not to hear the rumble of her stomach. The mention of food was enough to set her mouth watering. 'Weren't you waiting on Francesca?' the question was out of her mouth before she could stop it, knowing that it would betray more than a passing interest in him.

'Who?'

'The girl you were talking to…'

'The brash American?'

'Yes, the brash American,' Mason replied with a laugh at the apt description of her friend.

'No, she turned her attentions to a duke when she realised I wasn't interested.'

He'd moved slightly, subtly, without her noticing, so that he was now clearly within her line of sight. His eyes grazed a little too long over her features, but not in an unpleasant way. It sent sparkles spreading across her skin, and down into a stomach that was now past the 'growling' stage, and quickly moving on to the 'eating itself' stage.

'Food would be good. Though we're not going to find anywhere open. It's nearly midnight on New Year's Eve.'

'They'll open for me,' he said confidently.

'Why? What's so special about you?'

'I'm a prince,' he said with all the arrogance the title implied.

The sound of her laughter still rang in Danyl's ears as they picked their way through silent, snow-covered streets, his personal bodyguard hanging a suitably invisible distance behind. It wasn't that no one else had ever laughed at him before, at least not since he'd met Antonio and Dimitri. It was the laugh itself. A sound so pure, so unbridled, that the only thing that matched it was the joy expanding in his chest. There was something about the fiery young woman. She was like a present that he wanted to unwrap. Slowly.

Even bundled up in the thick winter wool coat she wore, she seemed impossibly small. Something that clearly suited her chosen occupation. How on earth she was able to wrestle control over a powerful thoroughbred, he couldn't fathom, but somehow he relished the chance to discover. The thought fired the blood in his veins and he silently cursed himself. He should know better. But as a stray tendril of that honey-brown hair escaped the confines of where she'd pushed it into the collar of her coat, he desperately wanted to sweep it back, just to feel the silken smoothness of it.

He let her lead him through the streets, almost sure she didn't have a particular destination in mind, especially when she paused at a crossroads, looked up and down, and as if at the last moment decided on a left-hand turn.

'So where in Australia are you from?'

'Ah, well done. Americans often mistake my accent for English somehow. The Hunter River Valley. It's in New South Wales.' The longing in her voice prompted his next question.

'You miss it?'

She looked up at him with a smile that was both wondrous and a little sad.

'Yes.' She shrugged her slim shoulders in the overly large winter coat. 'This is…strange, and… unfamiliar—but oddly familiar if you know what I mean? Too many TV shows, I suppose.'

She scrunched her nose up as she chose her words. He liked it. It was cute. Though he couldn't remember liking *cute* before.

'New South Wales is beautiful. And open. Not like…' She gestured with her hands towards the tall buildings around them in explanation.

'It takes a while to get used to.'

'Different to where you're from?' she asked, cocking her head to the side, as if trying to work something out about him.

'Yes, very different to Ter'harn,' he replied, putting stress on the name of his country.

'And Ter'harn is…?'

'On the African continent. But it has the benefit of

being a coastal country, so has deserts, mountains and a seafront.'

'What more could you want?' she asked, smiling, stirring the pit in his stomach.

I could want not to go back. I could want not to take the throne.

But he didn't say those things. He never said those things.

'So why are you here in New York?' he asked instead of voicing his secret thoughts. Because he was genuinely concerned that she'd somehow be able to pull them from the vault he kept them in.

'To study, train and learn. I'm going to be a jockey,' she said with pride. Genuine pride, not embarrassment or shame, not coy. 'My father trained some of the best riders in the world.'

'And he trained you?'

'Oh, God, no,' she said, laughing easily again. 'He wanted me as far from professional riding as possible. But I had the bug. I *have* the bug. He…gave up a lot for me. And though he might not have wanted me to ride, I see how proud he is when I win. It's a legacy and I want to live up to it.'

For a moment he wondered if someone in the palace might have put her up to this. But there was nothing in those eyes apart from truth. And suddenly, he was just a little jealous. He'd give almost anything to feel that way about being a future ruler. To want it, to want to be good at it. He wondered if he ever would.

They rounded the corner and found themselves at Washington Square Park, still open even at this time of night. It was littered only with the die-hards, freezing their backsides off in the middle of winter. He was about to ask about her mother when she spun around to face him.

'So what do I call you?' she asked, rubbing the bite of the cold winter air from her hands. 'My liege? Your Highness? O Great One?' she asked, turning back to cross the road, leaving him standing in a stream of her gentle mockery.

'Danyl's fine,' he said with a laugh as he caught up with her. 'And you?'

'Mason,' she tossed over her shoulder as she walked through the iron fencing around the park. She'd been marching ahead at such a pace, he almost walked into her as she pulled up short to look at the figures playing chess.

'Chess!' she exclaimed wholly unnecessarily, though he enjoyed the sheer delight in her voice. 'I've always wanted to play but I never had time to learn. Not with all that was needed doing on the farm.'

'Lucky,' Danyl replied. 'My father made me play almost every night. He would spend hours preaching the importance of each piece, valuing the Knight above all others and how it could teach me to be a better ruler.' She'd turned to look at him and narrowed her eyes at his tone. Could she sense the slight bitterness he tried to hold back from his words?

She turned back to the players—old men sitting at the small tables, chessboards etched into the surfaces, wrapped in layers clutching steaming cups—and Danyl felt oddly nostalgic.

'My father gave me a set when I left to come here for university.'

'That's lovely,' she said with a gentle appreciation.

'He kept back the Black Knight,' Danyl amended drily.

She laughed a little and stepped back towards him. 'I think that's sweet,' she decreed.

'I think it's silly,' he responded, taking a step closer to her, bringing him into the warmth she emanated, that slight trace of lime and bay he'd caught earlier.

Mason looked up at the Prince before her, wondering at the ease that had descended between them. The laughter he drew from her, the memories. Usually she was much more self-contained, 'closed off' as Francesca had complained once. But walking with him, talking to him…it felt as if she were a different person, as if she were being her true self, but better. It was a strange feeling.

From the streets and out of the surrounding buildings, voices began to cry out. The countdown to the New Year had begun. The cries rose up around them, breaking into the moment of silence Mason might have held for ever. They were standing so close she could feel the heat from his body.

Ten, nine, eight…

He was so much taller than her, she had to angle her head back to look up at him. Rather than making her feel small, as her diminutive height usually did, it made her feel protected, surrounded by him.

'Would it be inappropriate for me to kiss you at midnight?' he asked. His voice, lower and huskier than it had been before. She felt, rather than saw, his palms flatten out against his legs, as if he were preventing himself from reaching for her. Until she gave him permission. Until she allowed it.

She shrugged her shoulder as the subtle tension that had hummed between them since leaving the Langsford built to fever pitch. Her heart was pounding in her chest.

The way it had been as she'd led them further away from
the hotel. It increased as the time to midnight decreased.
Was she really going to let a prince kiss her?

Seven, six, five...

'I suppose it's not as if you're spoilt for choice,' she replied, looking around them briefly at the few groups that
had spilled onto the roads around the park, before being
pulled back to his gaze—the one that had not left her.

'There's always a choice, Mason.'

Four, three two...

He was giving her an out. He knew it, she knew it. But,
looking into his deep smoked-whisky-coloured eyes, she
thought she might drown, thought she might not be able
to breathe if she didn't take the chance...the chance to
act on the heady desire sparkling between them.

In answer to his question, she reached up to his tie and
gently tugged his head down towards hers.

One.

His firm lips pressed against hers, sending a thousand
little bursts across her skin...but it wasn't enough. As his
tongue gently swiped over her bottom lip, flames licked
up her spine and shivered out over her entire body. Another swipe begged entry, a third demanded it, and she
opened her mouth and met his tongue with hers. Her
hands came up to the lapels of his coat, pulling him towards her, clinging to them as if she could no longer stand
on her own two feet. Need and desire almost crushed her.
Adrenaline poured through her veins as she pulled him
deeper into a kiss she would never forget.

CHAPTER THREE

December, present day

'YOU DIDN'T LEAVE me with much choice.'

'There's always a choice. You told me that once, remember?' His own words, spoken in her Australian tones, echoed across the ten years almost to the day since he'd spoken them.

'Will you put the gun down now? Or are you really going to shoot me?' he asked.

'It's tempting. What are you doing here?' Mason asked, *without* the accompanying sounds of her putting the gun away.

'Can I turn around?'

'Slowly.'

'Slowly? For heaven's sake, would you put it down before you hurt yourself? Or worse, *me*,' Danyl said as he made a very slow turn on his feet.

'I'm not stupid, I do know how to use—'

Danyl pushed the barrel of the gun away from both of them, leaned in, grabbed the toe of the gun with his palm and pushed up, effectively releasing her grip whilst tangling her arms up in each other. He pulled the shotgun towards him slightly, breaking her hold, and dropped it to the floor. The resulting force, however, brought her forward against him, and left her flush along his chest.

He didn't know what angered him more, that she could have hurt herself, or that his body hadn't got the message his head had spent the better part of ten years telling him. He let the former win the silent mental argument.

'Are you mad?' he demanded, his voice cutting through the miles of silence around them. 'If that had gone off by accident, you would have just shot a prince!'

She peeled herself from his chest as if he were something contagious, muttering under her breath. He was pretty sure she'd just said that it would have been worth it.

He bit back the answering growl that threatened to emerge from his throat. Pushed down a voice that reminded him that he had stared down leaders of some of the world's greatest economies, he had resolved international disputes that could have escalated into all-out warfare, and that he should be able to handle one wayward Aussie jockey. Even if she had once broken his heart.

'Is there any coffee left? I've been travelling for hours to get here.'

'No coffee. No fire. I put it out before I knew it was you.' There was a distinct lack of sympathy in her tone. 'I'll ask again. What are you doing here, Danyl?' The sigh that left her lips sounded far too emotional for a simple, polite enquiry.

'You haven't replied to my parents' invitation to the gala.'

In the shards of moonlight peeking through the clouds racing across the night sky, he saw an archly raised eyebrow.

'You came all this way to find out if I'm attending a party?'

'Yes,' he ground out between clenched teeth, aware of just how stupid it sounded.

'Of course! Silly me. I'll just pop onto my private jet, fly halfway round the world, deck myself out in a pretty dress, smile for the cameras and then leave. No biggie.'

Mason could tell that he was surprised by her sarcasm. And perhaps the sting of acidity threaded through her words too. When they had first met, he'd encountered her fire, her youthful joy, her optimism. But Mason didn't think that she'd met him with the layer of sarcastic self-defence she'd developed in the years since. There were so many reasons she couldn't go to the palace, but the one she'd given wasn't any less valid than the others.

She turned back to the remnants of the fire and the large felled tree trunk that lay beside the damp, smoking ash, lowering herself to sit on the bark as delicately as any born princess would take to the throne. That he stayed standing irritated her, but was something she should get used to, she chided herself. She had long ago lost the right to stand beside him.

'This gala is important to my parents. It is quite likely to be the last that they hold as rulers of Ter'harn.'

'They're stepping down?' Mason asked, looking at Danyl not as the young, rakish playboy she'd once known, nor as the man before her, but as a royal. His image had refracted over the years, reformed into that of a king. It made her feel…sad.

'They are discussing it. And as such it is absolutely vital that it is perfect,' he stated, and the hard, determined look in his eyes made him into the powerful man lauded in the press as one of the future 'Kings to Keep an Eye On', as one particular paper had remarked. It washed away any memories of the man-child she had once known. Even back then there had been traces of Danyl's search for perfection. Hints at his need to be the unblemished, practically perfect in every way, figure-head for his parents. For his country.

'Veranchetti has been brought to the palace in Ter'harn. Even John is coming.'

Mason frowned. 'Is this what you want, or what your parents what?'

'Would it matter?' he asked.

Mason bit back the instinct to answer in the affirma-tive. It surprised her how much it did matter. Instead she focused between the lines. 'So even a prince must bend to a queen?' she asked.

The effect was instantaneous. His shoulders spread as his spine straightened, his head rearing back just slightly to allow him to view her from above his proud nose. 'No. But I do bend to my mother,' he conceded, his words muddying the arrogance in his stance just a little.

'I wouldn't know about that,' she said, the words ris-ing unbidden.

'No, I'm sorry. I didn't mean...'

'It's okay. I get it. I'd do anything for Pops. Which is why I can't come to the gala.'

Finally he took a seat opposite the dark black pit where the fire had once been.

'There's too much going on at the farm at the mo-ment,' she said, trying to explain, reaching for a reason he might understand and not question.

'It's just for a couple of days,' he interjected.

'And your time is more valuable than mine?' Mason felt the frustration rise within her, and she grasped it with both hands. It was much better than the pain that was lying just beneath.

'Yes. Actually, it is,' he replied with sincerity.

She fought the urge to hit him.

'Look, I'm not saying no, I'm saying I *can't*.' She couldn't quite bring herself to admit that she couldn't afford to leave the farm right now. But aside from the financials…aside from the practicality of it all… Just being near him was threatening to undo her.

She could smell him, that particular, unique all-male scent that was at once familiar and yet so very raw and new. She wanted to push him away. Push away the memories, the hurt…the pain. Threatening to break her heart all over again.

Danyl let that lie for a moment. There were a few twinkling red embers that were stubbornly clinging on to life in the remains of the fire between them. He watched them flare out in a dying breath as if they, like his options, were losing the battle.

'What are you doing out here?' he asked, realising then that he'd not even queried Joe McAulty, when they'd met back at the ranch-style home.

He could almost see her consider her words, picking and discarding ones that would get rid of him sooner.

'A couple of weeks ago a storm blew out some of the fencing, and I've come to replace a couple of the posts.'

'You brought the posts up here on your horse?' he demanded as if she were mad.

'Don't be silly,' she dismissed. 'One of the hands brought them out here in the ute a couple of days ago and left them up by the fencing. I just need to put them in.'

He knew that there was more to this trip than what she was saying, but he wasn't about to push her. Not now.

'It's a beautiful place. Just as you described it.'

'Thanks,' she said, that small smile playing with the edges of her mouth. 'You should see it during the day.'

'You should see the desert.'

Her eyes cut him with accusation and hurt and he had to look away.

'It's late,' she said, getting to her feet. 'I've got to be up early to get the posts in and get back.' She looked over to the horse he'd ridden in on and frowned as she took in the sight. 'If you're staying, then I'd suggest you put up a tent now, rather than later.'

He gave her a look that he figured had the power to fell at least ten men.

'What?' she asked, innocence or mock-innocence, he couldn't quite decipher.

His silence was enough.

'Ah,' she replied, and for the first time the small paltry smiles she had met him with evolved into something broad, something beautiful, and it stole his breath. 'I'm going to assume that Pops tried to give you a tent and you refused it because you believed that I'd just pack up and come with you.'

Danyl's jaw clenched, clearly enough of a response to answer her question. 'Well, there's a horse blanket at least, which I suppose is a good thing.'

'Why's that?'

'Because you're going to need something soft to land on when you fall off that high horse of yours. There's wood and kindling if you want to start a fire. But I'm going to bed. In my tent. Alone.'

Danyl watched her duck through the unzipped opening of the one-person tent, a thread of concern winding its way through his body. Not because he had to sleep outside under the stars. He'd done that more times than he could count back in Ter'harn. It was December, almost the height of summer here in Australia, so it was certainly no hardship. No, he was disturbed as much by what she did say as didn't. As he untied the bags from the saddle and saw to the horse, he calculated the time difference between Australia and Ter'harn, and then realised it didn't matter.

She had asked why the gala was so important. But she didn't get it. It wasn't just the gala. It was everything. It had to be perfect. He couldn't afford to mess up again. Because the last time he'd messed up, he'd almost lost hold of everything that he held dear.

As he unpacked his satellite phone, he knew what had to be done. He'd get his men to look into everything they could find out about her, because he wanted to know what Mason McAulty needed. Because everyone needed something. Sometimes, though, it just wasn't what was wanted.

Sweat dribbled down between Mason's shoulder blades, the muscles around them burning up to fever pitch. Hot, soaked and aching, she felt like a guilty schoolgirl for slipping out of the camp and down to the fencing before Danyl could wake up.

Dealing with him last night had been hard enough, but in the cold light of morning? How much more was one woman expected to take? Her stomach growled in accusation, calling her both a coward and indecently irresponsible for attempting such hard work without breakfast. The energy bar she'd consumed almost whole about an hour ago was not enough fuel for her body. Instead, she channelled her frustration as she hit the large block hammer onto the wooden post, so nearly in place.

Two more over-the-shoulder hits and she kicked against it to test its stability. Done.

She turned to find Danyl standing two feet behind her, looking horrifyingly good after what could only have been a hard night's sleep. And worse, he was armed with coffee and a smile. The smell hit her hard and her mouth started to water. From the coffee, she told herself. The coffee, not the man.

'Can I help?'

She allowed the shocked laugh its wings and it spread out before them like a challenge.

'A prince doing hard labour?' she scoffed.

'I can handle it,' he said with a shoulder-shrug.

'Sure, there's a spare block hammer over there,' she said, gesturing to the large canvas bag holding the tools. 'Square peg, square hole,' she added, and nodded to the gap in the fencing, one over.

He held out the coffee to her, which she stared at suspiciously before taking a sip. The moment the liquid hit her tongue she laughed.

'It's not burnt.'

'Of course not,' he said, sounding offended.

'There was a time when you thought coffee was made in shops, not grown and ground.'

'That was a long time ago.'

She took too large a mouthful and scalded her tongue.

She watched him retrieve the block hammer and approach the post as suspiciously as she'd approached the coffee. Mason nearly choked when he pulled off his T-shirt.

Admittedly, it was already stiflingly hot at seven-thirty a.m., but she hadn't had the time to steel herself against the image of his naked chest and the thoughts and memories that crashed against her. But this wasn't the chest of the young guy she had met ten years ago.

This was the chest of a man.

Powerful, toned, taut where it should be, and sweet lord, but the most delicious line of hair leading beneath a pair of jeans that should be outlawed on him. She felt like a voyeur, but couldn't move, couldn't take her eyes off Danyl, as he positioned the post in the hole with something like ease in comparison to the grunts, sweat and curses she'd needed to do exactly the same job.

But when he started to swing the hammer, *that* was when it got bad. All the muscles in his back undulating beneath his bronzed skin, more than a few shades deeper than when they had been in New York ten years before. The thought of how he had possibly obtained an all-over-body tan struck images and fantasies in her mind, one after the other with each blow to the post. And there she was, watching him and sipping coffee like some English aristocrat perving on the hired help. The irony wasn't lost on her.

Danyl ignored the gaze he knew was firmly fixed on his back. Or tried to at least. He felt it as a solid thing, an actual touch across his flanks and spine. And damn him if there wasn't a part of him that was preening beneath it.

Good. It was good that she was affected as much by him as he was by her. He'd had eighteen months to get used to the adult Mason McAulty, and still it wasn't enough. Oh, he could appreciate the way that her body had grown into itself, her face losing some of the softness he'd once enjoyed so much, to gain cheekbones and definition he knew some women would spend hours and hundreds of dollars of make-up trying to replicate. She'd always had an immaculate body—toned, smooth planes of skin, with every ounce of fat banished by the gruelling training needed for her to be able to compete at championship level. In fact, if anything, over the last few months she'd clearly lost too much weight, making him want to tie her down and force-feed her the sweet cream scones he remembered she loved so much.

Pushing the images that thought conjured up away from his mind in case he missed the post with the blunt end of the hammer and looked even more foolish than he probably did already, he decided to get down to business.

'What will it take to get you to the gala?'

'Nothing you can provide, I assure you.' There was more stubbornness in her words than arrogance. Perhaps there was even a trace of fear. Good. It would do her well to be suspicious for what he was going to hit her with. His aide had called him barely an hour ago, with news that had determined Danyl's course of action.

'Not even one million Aussie dollars?'

'If it were just about money, I'd be out there finding another race.' Her quick response suggested that she'd expected him to try and offer her money.

'You don't need to race, Mason. You could do just one of the interviews that the American press want and get that money in your account.'

'An interview? And the photoshoots? And the snide questions about my miraculous comeback? And *those* rumours?' Her voice was gaining both in righteous indignation and speed. 'Do you have even one iota of understanding as to how painful that would be for me? That even after all these years, and those three wins, people still want to know what happened with Rebel? It doesn't even matter that Harry and I were found innocent. The horse was drugged. I was accused of being involved. I was accused of *taking drugs*,' she said on a harsh whisper, as if even out here she didn't trust someone not to be listening. 'And there's nothing we can do about it.'

'It still hurts?' he asked, finally putting down the hammer and turning to her.

'It *all* still hurts, Danyl.'

'I—'

'Don't.'

She was closing him down. Just as she had done when she pushed him away before. When she pushed him out of her life. This time, he'd let her. This time when she did, he was going to make sure it was for the last bloody time.

As if sensing his own thoughts, she attempted to explain.

'It's just…there's too much work on the farm. Pops isn't as young as he used to be, but he won't let anyone other than me help with the running of it.'

'If your father needs as much help as you say he does, then I can find someone who'll be able to help. But I don't think that it's your father who has the problem.'

'What do you mean?' she asked, her voice laden with more than a little warning.

'Look, you trained for eighteen months, won three races, came back and stuck your neck in the proverbial sand. Is it possibly not just your father that's refusing help? One million dollars. I can have that in your account by this afternoon.'

'Money,' she practically growled. 'That's your answer to everything, isn't it?' she demanded.

'No, it's not payment. It's a charitable investment.' He

ignored the sarcastic huff of her laughter, and pressed on. 'As for the gala, I'll pay for all related costs, travel, clothing.'

'Don't be facetious.'

'I'm not,' he said, finally allowing through some of the tiredness and exhaustion that had been dogging him ever since the moment she'd approached the Winners' Circle eighteen months ago. 'As much as I hate to say this, it's not about you and me. It's for my mother. The gala's guests are some of the most famous, influential figures from around the world. And it's important that you look the part. So I will invest in your father's business, provide money that will keep you going for at least the next five years, I will get you on that private jet, and clothe you in whatever you need because that is what will make my parents' last event perfect. That is what will make them happy.'

He watched her quick mind make the calculations. About what she and her father could do with one million dollars. He could see, then, that he had her. Despite the pain, or in fact because of it. He could tell that Mason was hurt and confused, but that she simply couldn't refuse what he was offering her. And if that made him feel like a bastard, so be it. He needed this gala event to be perfect for his parents. Their last official act as rulers of Ter'harn.

'So, would you come with me?' he asked.

Mason nodded, her head lowered into her chest as if in defeat. And finally he felt relief. Because, once she'd come to the gala, she could leave and, aside from numbers on a banking balance sheet, she'd be out of his life for ever.

CHAPTER FOUR

February, ten years ago

'WOULD YOU COME with me?' Danyl asked.

'Where?' Mason replied.

'Back to my apartment,' he said, and she thought for a second that she heard a hint of nerves unusual in the amusingly autocratic royal.

This was it, she thought. The 'third date'. Over the last month they had explored Manhattan, every tourist attraction they could find, some of the most incredible out-of-the way restaurants, and tonight the opera. She'd been stunned by the opulence, but more so the music. She'd heard bits and pieces over the years, but to be there, to feel the air vibrate with the passion and power of the singers, it had been incredible. It had been a magical evening, and no, she didn't want it to end.

Danyl held his hand out to hers, the smile on his face one of excitement and perhaps promise. She couldn't help but return it, her lips curving upwards shyly, and she took his fingers in hers. He led her further down the block towards his apartment, rather than the car that had, on previous occasions, taken her back to the training facility where she shared a room with Francesca. She wondered what her friend would say, and then realised that Francesca probably wouldn't notice, being so consumed with her current *homme du jour*, as she liked to call them.

Somehow in this last month, Danyl had become an integral part of her life outside of training. Every spare minute she had, he was there. And when he wasn't? He would text or call, wondering what she was doing, what she was thinking. Mason had never experienced anything like it. As the only daughter to Joe McAulty, she had been treated with a distant reverence by the guys on the farm—none willing to incur her father's wrath or lose their job with anything more familiar. And with all the things to do on the farm she'd not had a huge amount of free time to explore life outside the estate.

With Francesca spending more and more time away from the training facility, Danyl had easily filled the gap. And she was glad. Because…she loved spending time with him. Listening to him, peppering him with questions about Ter'harn, his studies…anything she could think of to hear him speak in deliciously accented tones that ran shivers across her skin.

With her hand in his, and the other picking up the pretty skirts of the only dress she owned, Mason stepped into the foyer of Danyl's apartment block. Instinctively she wanted to wrap the thick woollen coat around her, to hide from the open perusal of the concierge, but Danyl simply led her determinedly to a lift slightly to the left from the main bank.

As they waited, she realised that Michaels, Danyl's personal guard, had hung back out of the way. Catching his discreet retreat, she called out to him, fishing in her pocket for the small bottle of lozenges she had promised him.

'Michaels, catch!' She threw the bottle across the short distance and he caught it one-handed, raising a smile through her nerves.

The lift doors opened and Danyl stepped in, bringing her with him.

'What was that?' he asked.

'A probiotic for his throat. It's amazing, but you can't get it in the States and I had some left.'

'Plying my staff with illegal medication?' He raised an arch eyebrow, but the humour in his tone softened the chastisement.

'Not illegal, just hard to get,' she replied, fighting with her nerves at being in such a confined space with a man who had driven her almost out of her senses over the last month. But tonight had been different. The other times they had met, it had been during the day, surrounded by New Yorkers and his personal guard. But something had changed under the cover of darkness, and she felt him weave a very slow, but very intense, seduction over her. She felt the heat of his gaze lap against her body, despite the layers of clothing between them.

She almost breathed a sigh of relief as they left the confined space of the lift and passed through the front door to his apartment. And then the sigh got caught in her throat.

From the sitting room, which included an open-plan kitchen that had clearly never been used, she wandered— because she *could* wander—along the wall lined with bookshelves, packed full of books of various genres, some she'd read and some she'd never heard of. It was so different from the little room she shared with Francesca, which was more like a backpacker's hostel than anything else. Danyl's apartment most definitely beat bunk beds and a communal kitchen.

At the end of the bookshelf wall was the most incredible view of Central Park she'd ever seen. Large windows let in the kind of vista usually viewed from a TV screen. The Jackie O Reservoir winked out from the middle, and somewhere down there was the famous Loeb Boathouse. Mason's fingers reached out to the cold glass as if she could touch the powerful grey clouds threatening to release little snow bombs on New York.

'The view isn't bad. But it's not as good as the sight of the desert in Ter'harn.' She couldn't help but laugh at the pride in his voice. But then the atmosphere changed. And she turned to find him looking at her.

'I wanted to ask about Scott, and didn't really know how to, so...' He let the sentence hang in the air between them.

'Oh, that,' she said on a breath. For a moment she'd thought he was going to talk about them, if there was even a 'them'...she'd thought he was going to let her down gently. Explain how a prince couldn't be involved with a commoner, let alone an Australian one.

Refocusing her thoughts, she felt her eyes narrow, squinting as if trying to see the way through to the right words. 'I didn't see him for a few days after the party. And, when I did, he was full of apologies. Said he was so drunk that he couldn't really remember much apart from the nearly broken nose and the fact that he knew it was the least he deserved. Us jockeys sometimes can't hold our alcohol because of the training.' Her words were met with a raised eyebrow, but she ploughed on. 'And he said to thank you for stopping him from doing something that he would have regretted.'

'Are you scared of him?'

She gave the question consideration. 'No. I'm not.'

'Do you think he'll try it again?'

'No,' she said confidently.

'With someone else perhaps?'

She shook her head. 'I spoke with Harry—our trainer. I just wanted to let him know to keep an eye out... He asked me if I wanted to make a formal complaint. And he *really* asked me. He's not just a friend of Pops, he's determined that female jockeys have a place in racing, and that nothing should interfere with that. Not even male egos,' Mason said with a smile and a gentle dig.

'Some male egos are warranted,' he said with mock superiority.

'It was a drunken pass that I wasn't open to. That's all. But I'm not naïve, and in case there is anything more to it then Harry knows now, as do the rest of the staff, and they'll be watching.'

'Good. Shall I order some dinner? What do you—?' His phone rang, cutting him off mid-sentence. He glanced at the number. 'I have to take this, sorry,' and he disappeared into a room.

Mason shucked out of her coat, walked over to the small kitchen and opened the perfectly stocked fridge. She checked a few cupboards and with an ear out for Danyl decided that he might be some time. Her fingers itching for something to do, she started the kettle to boil and began putting together what she'd need. There was smoked salmon, capers and cream. Perfect for a simple pasta dish and for avoiding any thoughts of what would happen next.

She thought of the small gift she'd impulsively got for him that was presently burning a hole in her pocket, and wondered again whether she should give it to him or not. But the moment she'd seen it she knew—or had done at the time—that it was perfect. Only now…she was beginning to think that perhaps it was foolish. That perhaps it was too soon for gifts, or for feeling like she was falling headlong into something she wasn't sure was even possible.

'Okay, I've got it. Thanks… Yeah. Love you too,' Danyl said, shutting off the call. Every time they spoke these days, reluctance and something defiant swirled in his chest. He had almost two terms left of his studies, and couldn't help the feeling that time was running out. Time for him to be…just Danyl, not Sheikh Danyl Nejem Al Arain. Time with his friends…time with a beautiful, dark-haired Australian beauty, who made him laugh, and who was comfortable enough in her own skin to laugh at him. Because when he went back to Ter'harn he knew it would be for the last time. It would be as the future ruler, with no room for error or mistakes. His whole life had been, and would be, about how he would serve and please the people of his country. He'd always known that, and he'd always respected that. But even so, he couldn't quite ignore the small, kicking and screaming voice that asked about pleasing himself.

'I thought we could—' He rounded the corner to find the breakfast bar laid with plates, cutlery, wine glasses and the most delicious-smelling pasta. 'Where did that come from?' he asked, genuinely intrigued.

'The fridge,' Mason responded with a laugh.

'There's food in the fridge?' He opened it—probably for the first time in four years—and was surprised to see it fully stocked. 'There's food in here?'

'It's where the plebeians usually keep it, Your High-and-Mightiness.'

'You cook?'

'Just sit and eat, Danyl, before you dig yourself even further into a hole,' she commanded.

He took a bite of the pasta and groaned. 'This is really good.'

'Do you want a shovel?'

'For the food?'

'For the hole!'

He tried to swallow past the laughter. Aside from occasionally sharing a meal with Antonio and Dimitri, he usually ate takeout alone, reading over either coursework or state papers.

'Was that your parents?'

'On the phone? Yes. I think they want me to go back to Ter'harn as soon as my course finishes,' he told her, the food cooling instantly in his mouth.

She gave him a small smile. 'And what do you want?'

'I...' He sighed. Whether it was Mason or the food casting a spell on his usual ability to deflect such questions, he couldn't tell. 'I'm not sure I'm ready. My parents, they're the best thing that ever happened to Ter'harn. Under their rule, our country has flourished. And...well, they're so perfect, I'm just not sure I can live up to them. I feel this...pressure to be as good as them,' he finished with a shrug. But the movement of his shoulders was only part of what he felt...helpless. The other part, the darker part, was more difficult. But there was something about Mason McAulty that made him think she might understand, might somehow help? 'I don't know what kind of ruler I'll be. I can't see how...how I'll be able to make the decisions in the same way that my father has. How I will find the right answers to problems the way my father has.'

She looked at him, her deep, walnut-coloured eyes shining up at him with sympathy, but also a ruefulness that surprised him. 'You won't and you can't.'

Danyl's head reared back at the unexpected answer he felt like a slap. Until she pressed on.

'You're not your father, Danyl. You must find your own way to make your own decisions. Your own answers to different problems.'

Danyl felt something like panic. He heard an inner voice left over from childhood insecurities and child-hood fears… *What if I can't?*

He didn't realise that he'd said it out loud until she placed her hand on his arm, the weight and warmth of it grounding him, blocking out that voice.

'But you can,' she assured him, an easy smile making the weight of the conversation a little lighter. 'Making a decision is easy. It may not always be the right one, and it may not always be perfect. The decision is the easy bit, as long as you don't let your fear overwhelm you.'

He looked at Mason, taking her in, the long swathes of brown curls falling around her shoulders, but it was her eyes. The defiance, the strength, the determination in those dark brown orbs that sang to him on the air about them.

'It is that easy? Just decide not to be overwhelmed?'

'The decision? Yes. Doing it?' Her lips curved up-wards. 'Not so much. But that's what makes it worth it. If it was easy, everyone would do it.'

'Is that how you approach riding?'

'A little. Any doubts, any fears I may have…they are kept firmly in my room. I can't approach a horse with any of those emotions because they would sense it, they would know. By the time I'm with my horse, my mind is set, my goal is clear and my mind is calm.'

Danyl let out a huff of laughter. 'I never thought I'd see a connection between the people of Ter'harn and a horse, but I believe that they would smell fear just as easily as a thoroughbred.'

'Why not? We're all, at some level, the same. We know when there is a threat, we can tell. Years of evolution hasn't trained the predator-prey dynamic out of us.'

'So, I must become the predator?'

'No.' The gentle laugh soothed some of the edginess of the conversation. 'But I imagine you have to approach ruling with that same separation between your private concerns and your public focus. You can only do the best you can. You are—despite being a prince—only human.'

Danyl was a little stunned. He'd never had a conversation about this with anyone. Not even Dimitri and Antonio. He'd never admitted how much he feared failing his parents, his country. But Mason hadn't dismissed his concerns as silly. Hadn't fawned over him, telling him that he was being silly. Instead she'd listened, understood and shared. And it felt as if some of that weight had been lifted. As if he could suddenly see a pathway into the future that wasn't necessarily treading in his father's footsteps, but making his own.

Mason had felt the honesty in his words, and was humbled by the fact he'd shared such a thing with her. 'I know a little about that pressure. Sometimes I wonder whether I'm riding for me or for my father. Don't get me wrong, I love it. There's nothing like riding, being…connected with the horse—it's like I'm flying. But…'

'Did you always want to be a jockey?'

'I know most young girls probably want to be…princesses,' she said, laughing and nodding to Danyl. 'But my mum left when I was two. And Pops gave up everything, gave up travelling around Australia, training some of the best horses in the country. He gave up what he loved for…'

'For someone he loved,' Danyl finished.

Mason was surprised. She'd not really looked at it like that before.

'Is that when you learnt to cook?'

'I had to! My dad could burn water.'

She could see that he wanted to ask more, about her mum, about her childhood, but she didn't want that. Not now. Not tonight. Instead, seeing that he'd finished with his plate of food, she went to her coat and retrieved the small gift.

'For you.' She presented it to him with a shrug, hated that it gave away her insecurity. To her surprise, his entire face lit up and stole her breath.

'A present? For *me*?' he asked, seemingly incredulous, and his reaction was completely at odds with the little package wrapped in cheap paper.

'I wasn't really sure what to get the Prince who has everything, but it's just a small thing.'

He eyed it with a reverence completely unnecessary for the small gift she'd chosen, but instead of opening it he simply held it in his hands, looking not at it, but at her. The smile he wore was the kind of smile that couldn't be faked. Not because it wasn't bright enough, or didn't reach his eyes, which it did. But because of how it made her feel. Something tight in her chest unfurled for the first time since she'd seen the present she was going to buy him. Something oddly like excitement. And she couldn't help but allow it to pull at the edges of her own smile.

Danyl brought it up between them and studied the shape with a rather surprising amount of concentration, given that his mind was very much on unwrapping Mason, rather than the present. His fingers traced the sides of the small rectangle-shaped box and frowned. He shook it, and her hand reached out to gentle his movements. 'Not too hard,' she said, laughing.

He was trying to decide whether the situation required careful release of the tape holding the colourful paper together, or if he could give in to the urge to tear it all away to reveal what she had brought him. He looked up and found her smiling as if she'd read his mind.

'Have at it, Your Highness.'

Impatience and a slightly childish glee filled him, and for possibly the first time in his life he did exactly what he was told. He tore away the paper, and pried open the thin card box, producing an object surrounded by bubble wrap.

This time he gently peeled back the last of the tape to reveal something that stole his breath.

It was a chess piece. A black-painted, hand-carved wooden Knight.

'I know it doesn't match the exquisite set you have...' she started apologetically.

'It's perfect,' he said, cutting in. And it was. It wasn't just the piece, or the fact that now he could finally play a game of chess after nearly four years... There was a thought drifting somewhere in his mind, deeply layered between incredulity and denial...it whispered to him,

suggesting that this was what his father had meant to
teach him. That it was Mason, not the Knight, that he
couldn't rule his country without.

'I'm speechless,' he said honestly.

'Perfect,' she replied, the delight shining in her eyes
as clear as the North Star.

'Now that we have a complete set, perhaps I can teach
you how to play. But I have to warn you—it might take
a really, really long time,' Danyl said, unable to stop the
smile pulling at the edges of his mouth.

'How long?' she asked as if they were both sharing
the same joke, the same thought.

'Hours. Days even. Maybe more. Are you okay with
that?'

'I think I'm okay with that.'

Big brown eyes looked up at him, unfathomable rich
coffee that made him want to lick his lips. He could see
the battle warring in them, the way he could feel it himself.

'We could start now…' he said, everything in him
screaming *no* as the suggestion took him further away
from what he really wanted. He got up from the couch
and went over to the chess board, placing the Knight in
its new place. He needed something to do with his hands
to prevent himself from reaching for her.

'What if I thought there was something else we could
be doing instead?' she asked. She was the devil, tempting him with the very thing he wanted, so, so much. 'And
if there was…' she said continuing with short little sen-
tences that spoke volumes, 'if there was…then I should
say that…' she was avoiding his gaze, a blush that rose
beneath his skin, still sun-kissed after months in wintry
New York, 'that I've never done this before.'

* * *

There. She'd said it. She'd had to force the words out through embarrassment and an odd mixture of shame, because she had never felt ashamed of being a virgin before. It wasn't really shame, she thought, struggling for the right word. It was more regret, because surely this would be the moment that the Prince finally woke up and realised that he shouldn't be playing with a girl that was effectively nothing more than a glorified stable hand. This was the moment that he would laugh, tell her that she shouldn't be playing dress up as an adult, that he didn't like silly virgins.

It was his silence that finally drew her gaze reluctantly back to his. It was as if he was waiting for her full attention.

'I am truly honoured that you would offer me such a gift.'

It took a moment for his words to sink in. He hadn't undermined her by asking her if she was sure. He hadn't second guessed her decision, a decision she hadn't made lightly. He didn't take away the power of her choice, and instead his next words gave over all control to her. Gave over himself to her.

'At any point, *any*, Mason, I will stop. It doesn't matter what we are doing, how far you think we may have gone. I will stop.'

She felt the truth in his words as a promise written against her skin. It was complete acceptance of her and who she was. And for the first time since she'd left Australia and come to New York, feeling overwhelmed and insecure, unsure of her choices and herself, when she was anywhere but on the back of a horse, this...*this* was the first time in months that she felt right, that she felt complete. The assurance, the faith that he would protect her, that he too wanted her with the same matched conviction and desire with which she wanted him, was the most intoxicating thing she'd ever felt.

She nodded to indicate that she'd understood what he was offering her, incapable of words, and rose to meet him where he stood. She reached for him then, wrapping her hands around his neck, his height such that she had to stand on tiptoe. Even then that wasn't quite enough for her to reach his lips. His arms outlined the sides of her chest, and she felt his fingers brush the sides of her breasts, through the thin silk of the top she was wearing. They traced the outline of her body, until they reached the hem, and he went to pull off the garment. She laughed as it got caught around her neck and pulled from his embrace to help remove it. In a second she was back in his embrace, returning her touch to his toned chest. She marvelled at the hard body encased in the finest cotton shirt, her roughened fingers catching on the fine threads. Her fingers dipped between the shirt buttons, relishing the feel of Danyl's smooth, hot skin and almost laughed again as he shivered the moment her cool hands met his torso. She slipped the buttons from their holes and pressed her lips against his chest, exalting at the feel of his skin against her mouth, her tongue. A growl rose from beneath her kiss and he pulled away, so that his mouth could find hers once more.

Sensation and desire and need all warred within her as he stepped backwards, leading her, unwilling or unable to break the kiss. They backed into the bedroom and the moment they were through the door, instead of heading to the bed, he spun her around so that she could feel his chest against her back, his arms around her waist holding him to her as if he didn't want to let go of her, of this moment. Her arms went up, once again, to meet behind his neck, pulling his head down to hers, as he pressed open-mouthed kisses across her shoulder, sending a cascade of shivers throughout her body. She felt his fingers at the clasp of her bra and it was quickly discarded. His hands came around to cup her breasts, the warmth of his palms soothing the tightness of her nipples. His fingers played across her skin, gently teasing groans of pleasure from her and building the throbbing between her legs. One hand dipped over the thin waistband of her silk skirt and threaded between her legs, her legs opening enough to let his palm press heavily against that desire.

'You will be my undoing,' he whispered into her ear, his tone dark and needy. She sucked in a breath of air that sounded desperate to her own ears as he flexed his hand between her legs. Sensations sparkled straight from her core, sending a flush across her skin.

'Open your eyes,' he commanded, and she reluctantly opened her drugged eyelids, not realising that she'd had them closed.

She looked straight into a mirror hung on the back of the bedroom door. And what she saw stole her breath.

She saw herself, her head back against his broad shoulder, his forearm across her naked breasts, as if protecting her modesty. Her long auburn hair ran like a waterfall across her shoulder, reaching almost halfway down to her waist. But it was the sight of his other arm, the one that covered the centre of her body, the hand retreating from between her legs, that made her want to cry out and tell him 'no'. She locked eyes with his in the reflection in the mirror, and caught the ghost of his smile as if he knew what she was thinking.

But his fingers were bunching the thin material of her skirts, bringing it higher across her thighs as if both teasing her and allowing her the time to put a stop to his movements. Her eyes flickered between his gaze and his hand, and all words, all thoughts stopped when he reached beneath her panties and trailed one long finger down to find her clitoris. She gasped out loud then, a violent shiver of pleasure rocking her body within his arms. Again and again he traced over the sensitive skin, until he plunged that same finger into the wet heat of her core. Her chest rose away from his, pushing her breasts into his hand, arcing from him and simultaneously allowing him greater access. Need coursed through her, the blood in her veins pounding in her ears, but not enough to mask the sounds of arousal falling from her lips. Sighs, groans, incomprehensible words littered the air as he plunged his fingers into her again and again, each time drawing her body against his, where she could feel the power of his erection behind her. She wanted…she wanted…so much it was impossible for her to tell.

'Open your eyes,' he commanded again.

But she shook her head where it rested against his shoulder. She couldn't, she dared not look at what he was doing to her. It would send her over the edge, she instinctively knew. This tightness, this need—it was overwhelming. It was building in her, begging for release.

'Please, Mason, I want to see you. I want to see it happen. Just let go and open your eyes. Let me give you this pleasure, let me show you what it can be,' he asked of her.

She opened her eyes, and met his once more in the reflection. The need she saw there, the desire…it was as if he too was as overwhelmed as she. His deft fingers plunged once more into her and her whole body rushed to meet them in an explosion. Stars, she saw stars, and brightness, and the last thing before she saw almost nothing was the look in his eyes, humbled and awed.

Her muscles clenched around his fingers, again and again as her body was rocked by the most intense orgasm. Her legs turned to jelly as his strong arm held her in place against his body. He turned her in his arms, sought her mouth and claimed her with a kiss that branded her with passion. She kissed him back with everything she had, everything she wanted to say but couldn't. It was as if he'd tasted her very soul.

He picked her up where she stood and walked over to the bed with her in his arms, laying her down gently on the bed.

'Remember what I said. We can stop. At any time.' The sincerity in his eyes was so much a gift she couldn't respond with words. She nodded instead, pulling him into a kiss. He broke it only long enough to remove his clothes, and the rest of hers.

She'd thought that the sight of him fully naked might make her nervous, might make her worried, but instead she only felt need. The need to give him what he'd given her, the need to find that incredible height she'd felt before she'd fallen completely. The need to join with him and take him inside her... He reached for a condom and she watched him roll it over the long, hard length of his erection. He lay beside her, his hands roaming freely over her shivering skin, over her breasts, over her toned thighs, between her legs once more. Mason didn't think it was possible to feel that desire again so quickly, but he teased it from her, once again bringing forth the sound of her pleasure, her need. She pulled him towards her, and instinct took over, somehow her body knowing what she wanted before the thought could enter her mind.

He braced himself on his forearms, either side of her head, locking his gaze with hers, as if desperate to see everything she felt, every tiny reaction her eyes might express.

She felt the tip of his arousal at her core and unbidden pleas rose to her lips; she wanted to feel him, inside her.

He entered her slowly, allowing her to get used to his size, to get used to the feel of him she wanted so much. It was strange, and for a moment slightly painful, stinging in a way she hadn't quite expected. His fingers came up to her face, smoothing across the planes of her cheeks.

'Okay?'

She waited and her body adjusted, welcoming him, needing him more. Her hips shifted beneath his, experimenting with the feel of him inside her.

'Very,' she said with a small smile, her hands tracing the length of his back, urging him deeper into her. She gasped as he filled her completely, an exquisite feeling she could never have imagined coming over her.

Before long, the slow, controlled movements weren't enough. She wanted so much more. She pulled him into her again, and he smiled, increasing his pace until he too was lost to all but sensation. His own sounds of pleasure increased hers tenfold and once more sparkles dusted her skin, sticking to it with the slick evidence of their need. He plunged into her, so fully, she felt that he had reached her soul, and the tension that had built impossibly between them reached a crescendo that she thought she might never recover from.

CHAPTER FIVE

December, present day

HER HEART WAS RACING, need and desire painted her skin with a flush, and her breathing was coming out in small pants. Mason opened her eyes, and closed them immediately. The plush cream interior of the private jet jarred against the dream memory of their first night together. She resisted the urge to groan aloud, knowing that Danyl would hear it from where he sat on the other side of the plane. It would be a miracle if he hadn't heard whatever sounds she'd made during the intensity of her dream. From that first night to their last, sex had never been a problem between them. If anything, it had been the glue to keep them together for that short while.

And then, as sorrow and loss crept into her consciousness like a thief, stealing pleasure and happiness, she desperately wanted to cling to that dream. To cling to that moment when they had been innocent, when they had had no fear of the future, no sense of reality about to come crashing down...no warning...

She fought the tears that were gathering at the edges of her eyes and instead tried to focus her mind on the present.

'Would you like some water?' Danyl asked, his tone dark, as if he had sensed her thoughts. He'd always somehow done that, but where once she'd loved him for it, now she resented it.

'What I'd like is a shower,' she bit back harshly. Too harshly.

From the moment her father had sealed her fate with the words *'You should go'* after they had returned to the farm and Danyl had explained his proposition, a whirlwind of activity had surrounded her, even though it was just the three of them in the house, Danyl's entourage having stayed outside with the vehicles.

Within fifteen minutes a small bag was packed with only the essentials, assurances that the right clothes would be provided her made, promises of financial transfers were given, papers—that Danyl had arranged to be emailed over—were printed out and signed, and Mason had found herself ushered onto a helicopter that ferried them to a small airfield where she was presented with the royal family's private jet.

She was wearing the same clothes she'd put on that morning, the sweet smell of hard work and horse clinging to her shirt the way the past had clung to her dream.

'Then by all means have one,' he said, not even bothering to look up from the laptop he had been punishing with an energy and determination that she had once relished.

'Really? You have a shower on a plane?'

'Sadly it's less a luxury and more a necessity these days.'

These days. As if at some point in his life he'd imagined something different. There were a million ways Mason had once dreamed of taking this trip with Danyl to Ter'harn. But never like this. She tried to be kind to the young woman who had thought that she might go to the palace as his fiancée. But she couldn't help the harsh thoughts that told her off for being foolish. As if she—a girl from a small town in Australia—might one day be the Princess of a desert kingdom. Things like that just didn't happen.

The sound of furious typing brought her attention back to Danyl. She'd feel pity for the person on the receiving end of his frustration, if she wasn't in exactly the same position. He'd changed. And yes, so had she, but looking at him then, the slight dusting of grey at his temples only serving to make him look even more sophisticated and self-assured, she could see that this was not a man who would dye away the signs of his age, but embrace them and harness them to his advantage. She remembered the sight of his chest as he'd pounded in the wooden stake a few hours and a few hundred thousand miles away. He had kept his lean, mouth-watering physique and somehow only added to it.

Mason wondered briefly what he saw when he looked at her. A lucky escape? Something inside her, buried deep, protested against the thought, but she forced herself to be practical. What they had had was ten years ago. Things changed. People changed.

Danyl waited until he'd heard her retreat to the back of the plane following the air stewardess, who was telling Mason where she could find towels, before risking a glance at her. He'd not been able to take his eyes from her while she was sleeping. Even though it was almost as painful as not looking at her.

Another email pinged into his inbox and he bit back a groan. Under any other circumstances an email with the subject line 'Last Chance!' with an eight-by-ten picture of a beautiful woman sent to a member of the royal family could be mistaken for a blackmail note. It almost felt like that from where he was sitting.

At the time, he'd thought hiring a private matchmaker was a good idea. If people thought it was hard meeting someone in this technologically driven, increasingly reclusive world, they should try being a prince. If he'd just wanted someone to grace his bed, that wasn't exactly a hardship, although he was mentally avoiding the maths on how long it had actually been since the last time he'd indulged his desires. It was the *perfect* someone he was looking for. The person who would become his Queen, who would stand beside him at royal and diplomatic functions, who would not have any expectations above that 'duty', who would allow his parents to step away from the throne and for him to finally take on the full mantle of royalty. Someone who would—eventually—provide him with heirs. And if that last thought bit a hole into the part of his heart he'd thought long since anaesthetised, then that was his problem, not hers. Whoever she may be. He scanned the email once more.

To: D.NejemAlArain@arascan.tu
From: AngelServices@email.com
Subject: Last Chance!
Danyl,
I have looked high and low to find you what you want, but I'm beginning to think that even you don't know what that is. In the last eighteen months I have provided you with a number of perfect candidates and you have either offended, dismissed or infuriated each one of them. Amata de Cayce will be present at your parents' gala.

She is a lovely girl. Perhaps too lovely for you, but she's your last chance. The end of your parents' gala will be the termination of our contract.

I will expect all finances to be settled by the end of the gala weekend.

He had to give Angelique her due. There was no real appropriate sign-off for that kind of email. Danyl suddenly felt as if he were nine years old, back in the palace's private school room, being told off by the sublimely superior Madame Fortier.

He ran a hand over his face, before clicking on the attachment of Amata de Cayce. Christ, he must be getting old, because the girl—and she looked like a girl—seemed so young, even though her stats put her at twenty-six. It was older than Mason when he'd first met her.

He bit back the growl of frustration that threatened to erupt from his chest. He should have told Mason that he had a date for the event. But it was not as if it was easy to slip into conversation: *I know I had to pay you an inordinate amount of money to come here, but I already have a plus one...* Nope. Wouldn't quite cut it. And besides, Mason was only attending at his parents' request, not his. Not really.

He fought the wave of thoughts cascading through his mind, then gave up and swam in their stream. He had to admit that it was ironic, his looking at the picture of a woman who *might* be his future bride, when the one he once thought *would* be was presently engaged in the shower and presumably trying to work out several ways in which she could either kill, maim or at the very least inflict some kind of damage to his royal person.

Then again, it was exactly because of the woman

presently engaged in the shower that he was forced to look for an unemotional, very heavily stringed but essentially perfect marriage of convenience. And then he was drenched in memories of Mason, of what they had had, what they had lost and what, now, could never be. Danyl was a practical man, and for the most part always had been. The only thing he could do was try to make the most of this ridiculous situation. He'd hated bringing Mason all the way to Ter'harn. He could see the hurt, the fear, lying hidden in those deep brown pools he'd once thought to drown in.

Mason had said that she'd refused the financial incentive of the interviews because they would zero back in on Rebel and the horse race that had effectively ended her career. Well, for eight years at least. She'd only come to the Winners' Circle, as he now knew, to be able to use the purse money to rescue her father's farm. And if guilt warred in his breast for thinking it was for fame, or money for personal gain, then that was his penance for thinking so badly of a woman he'd once…

He forced his mind back to the point. Rebel. He hadn't realised that she was still so haunted by it. In his mind, he scanned the press coverage of the Hanley Cup and realised that almost every single mention of her success had been grudgingly acknowledged in direct association with the events surrounding Rebel's death. It was in every article, and one enterprising journalist had even managed to get it into a headline.

Perhaps, if at the very least, getting to the bottom of what had happened that day might help lay the past to rest. Because the rest of it…well. Pain rose up to choke off the conclusion of that sentence. It would do them both good to draw a line under their past. Because he knew neither of them had been able to move on.

He listened for the sounds of the shower, making sure she was still there and wouldn't interrupt his next conversation.

He picked up the sat phone and waited for the connection to go through.

'Odir.'

'It's me, Danyl.'

'Danyl, good to hear from you. Everything okay?'

'Yes, well, as long as I survive the gala.' Danyl heard a chuckle from the ruling monarch of Farrehed. A sound that he'd once thought impossible from the imposing ruler of the neighbouring country.

'Did you not get our RSVPs? Sorry—the kids have been running rings round my secretary since the nanny went on holiday last week.'

An image of Odir's family sprang into Danyl's mind. When he thought about his future, he could never imagine himself being as lucky as Odir had been—even in spite of the rocky path he and Eloise had once been on. In fact, it was a minor miracle that Odir and Danyl had become so close, given Odir's father's illegal incursion onto Ter'harnese soil the night of Odir's wedding. It had taken weeks of intense negotiations to resolve, but working together had forged a bond that would not be easily undone again.

'RSVPs all received. Actually, I wanted to ask a favour.'

'Of course. I'll never refuse a chance to put you in my debt,' Odir joked, both men knowing full well that they were beyond debts.

'Can I borrow Malik? I want him to look into something for me, though I'm not quite sure what he'll be able to find, if anything. It was ten years ago, now, so...'

'If there's anything to find, he'll find it,' Odir assured him, and passed on Malik's contact details.

Mason emerged into the cabin, her skin hot and pink, not from the heat of a shower so good it should be illegal on a private jet, but from sheer fury. She'd just got off the phone with her father and she was trying so very hard not to hit Danyl. Hard.

'You got my father a woman?'

It was a beat. She might have missed it if she hadn't known him so well, but he'd definitely taken a beat. Enough time to look her up and down with hawk-like eyes that made her suddenly conscious of every single part of her body. She wanted to growl. He'd always had that way of distracting her. Instead, she focused back on the problem at hand.

'I got your father the best estate manager I could find.'

'And she's a woman.'

'Yes, Mason. The best estate manager around happens to be a woman.'

'Is this payback?'

'Payback for what?'

'I don't know. You never needed much to be petty.'

'Don't be silly. I'm not petty,' Danyl said with a trace of arrogant offence heavy in his tone.

'Yes, you are.'

'No, I'm not.'

'You are! You spent a week dressed in pink shirts because of the crack I made about real men wearing pink.'

'Well, it's true. Only a real man *can* wear pink. And besides, you said it brought out the colour of my eyes.'

'It brought out the colour of something,' Mason grumbled in reply.

'Is he unhappy with her?'

'What?'

'Mary. Is your father unhappy about her being a woman?'

'No, not really.'

'Well, then.'

And that, it seemed was the end of the conversation.

The armoured limousine glided through the palace gates with more grace than Mason could have thought possible when she'd first spied the vehicle waiting for them on the tarmac of the landing strip.

She'd been slightly disappointed that the private airfield was so close to the palace, having wanted to see Aram, a city she'd once heard so much about. But the moment the gleaming transport arrived at its destination outside the main palace entrance, all her yearning was forgotten.

'Karl, we're supposed to be using the left wing's entrance.'

'Sorry, Your Highness, but the sheikh and his Queen requested it.'

Mason was sure that the growl vibrating through Danyl's compressed lips was holding back a barrage of frustration and took perverse enjoyment that someone was playing Danyl at his own game for once.

The driver came round to her side to open the door, Danyl having swung his open and emerged from the dark interior before the driver could do anything but shrug his shoulders. It took a moment for her eyes to adjust to the bright light she had been shielded from by the limousine's tinted glass. So her first gaze upon the palace was one that slowly came into focus through a white glare, as if she was to be both physically and emotionally stunned.

It took her breath away. Quite literally. The large, sprawling palace before her was outlined in Moorish architecture. She caught glimpses of manicured gardens off to the left and right of the palace, and even from here she could smell honeysuckle and ginger, and see the riot of incredible colours coming from the immaculately cultivated gardens. The heat of the sun was gentle, but then they were that far from Australia now, where it was the height of summer.

'I don't know how you could have borne being away from this for so long,' she said, the words escaping her mouth unbidden.

'While I was in New York?' he queried. 'I knew this would always be waiting for me.'

So did I, her mind responded.

'And besides, you only see what the royal family want you to see. Not the hard work, the duty, the practicality of running a small kingdom alongside a prime minister and surrounding countries who either want to steal your country's products, or buy them at an undervalued price.'

'I thought you would have liked the cut and thrust of it, the power games and winning,' she returned.

'I'm good at it,' he replied. Which said enough.

The light from the sun, although more wintry, suited the pink ochre of the palace walls. Turrets, which Mason was pretty sure might not actually be called turrets, sprang up at different twists and turns of the building that sat above three layers of circular steps. At the top of which stood...

Oh, God, it was Danyl's parents.

The moment she caught sight of them she was plunged into ten-year-old fantasies. It was like a glimpse at a possible future that had never happened, and hurt all the more for it. Something she'd wanted so, so much that could never be. They would have come here, they would have been met by his parents, she would have been welcomed as his fiancée.

Her hand reached out to grasp the door handle, whether anchoring her to the past, or keeping her in the present, she could no longer tell. She saw her white knuckles, but couldn't feel anything past the blood rushing in her ears.

It was so much worse because back then she hadn't allowed herself to imagine this moment, as if self-delusion had attempted to protect her from what this moment would mean, how it would make her feel.

Danyl spoke her name, and when she looked at him she realised that he, too, was thinking the same thoughts. Because the compassion in his eyes was almost too hard to bear. Compassion and something horribly like accusation.

This is your fault, a little voice prodded at her conscience. And then she soothed it with a response. *It was no one's fault.* She'd done what she'd had to do. For both of them.

A uniformed member of staff somewhere behind the royal couple at the top of the stairs twitched as if she had made them all wait too long, as if she was indulging in negligent etiquette. The Queen's smile hadn't moved an inch, but her eyes darted between Mason and Danyl.

She felt Danyl's hand on her arm, guiding her up the stairs to meet the older couple. She'd seen pictures of them in the press throughout the years, and remembered them from photos that Danyl had once shared with her, a gleam of pride that even he couldn't disguise shining in his eyes.

And Mason felt a thread of awe and self-consciousness that she'd never experienced in Danyl's presence. Sheikh Hashid Nejem Al Arain, tall like his son, stood in a military stance that had him looking as if he were almost made of stone. But his eyes hid a deeper emotion. Hashid was polite, regal, but there was a gentleness about him that softened the rigidity of his appearance. Danyl's mother, Elizabeth, while poised and, Mason considered almost instantly, the true definition of exquisite, was, in almost direct contrast to her husband, what could be described as *touchy feely*. Mason found herself in a warm embrace, one held for a beat too long. Mason cast a frowned glance at Danyl over her shoulder, who seemed as unsettled by Elizabeth's warm welcome as Mason felt.

A pinprick of fear welled in her chest. Could she know? Would Danyl have told her?

But Danyl's slight shrug suggested that he was as confused as she.

'Elizabeth, put the poor girl down. She must be exhausted after the flight,' her husband commanded in almost accentless English, and from somewhere in her memory she fished the information that explained Hashid had attended Eton, and had been disappointed when Danyl had chosen NYU.

'We're so pleased that you could come to the gala. It's such a long way for you, but we really do appreciate it,' said the Queen, having almost reluctantly released Mason from her embrace. 'After all, it wouldn't be a true celebration of your incredible success at the Hanley Cup without you here.'

There was a flurry of activity over the Queen's shoulder, and Mason watched as the older woman schooled her features into something that managed to be both courteous yet simultaneously disapproving.

'Ah, yes. Danyl, your date for the gala arrived a few hours ago.'

Mason had prepared herself for this. She hadn't needed Danyl to tell her that he already had a plus one. It was only logical for a man on the hunt for a bride, if the newspapers were to be believed. Over the past eighteen months he'd been seen with a series of high-profile dates that had led to insatiable speculation of just who would win the Princess lottery. Speculation she had tried to remain firmly outside of. Because it hurt. Because it reminded her of all the things it might have been.

'Oh,' Mason said, turning to Danyl, hoping that her expression would be curious, rather than pained, 'is Birgetta here?' Deep down her money had been on the poised Scandinavian blonde she had seen pictures of him with at some Greek charity event a few months back.

'Who,' his mother interjected archly, 'is Birgetta?'

'Birgetta is…a friend,' he finished as if the word *friend* had left a bitter taste in his mouth. Mason almost felt sorry for him. Almost. 'I believe that she has run off with her personal assistant and is currently in the process of causing a bit of a ruckus on the Croatian coast.'

'Then who is…?' Mason trailed off, both because of the impertinence of the question, and because the flurry of activity behind the Queen had suddenly appeared amongst them.

'Danyl!'

A young blonde in an improbable amount of tulle and frills collapsed into the group, almost sending his parents scattering, launching herself and her big blue eyes right into Danyl.

'It's *so* good to see you!' she exclaimed, rushing into a stream of words so fast that Mason could only pick out the occasional syllable.

As Mason hung back she dared to cast a glance at Danyl, who seemed almost horrified by the sudden appearance of the young woman, the shock of it clearly robbing him momentarily of his ability to disguise his feelings. It was cruel to smile, because the young girl— though she was clearly totally inappropriate for him— had an uncontainable joy and enthusiasm about her. And for just a moment an ache formed in her chest, as she remembered that perhaps once she had been like that. So free and uninhibited.

Danyl called to a man over her shoulder and asked him to escort Mason to her rooms. She'd almost expected him to say 'chambers', but when she caught sight of who he'd asked she couldn't help the smile form on her lips.

'Michaels,' she said and just about stopped herself from greeting him with a hug, the way that she had almost ten years before. She felt rather than saw Danyl flinch, tension suddenly cutting through the air about them as if he recognised the moment she feared she'd given herself away.

'Miss McAulty. You look well,' Michaels replied and she couldn't help but smile at the bland pleasantry. She'd been dragged halfway across the world, was wearing rumpled jeans and a T-shirt and was currently only being held up by adrenaline and three hours' sleep.

'You are too kind,' she said, with a dryness that only made him smile more.

She suddenly felt out of her depth, alienated from the

decorum and the rules of etiquette she had never really known. And then she realised that she'd never seen Danyl in a royal setting, that their relationship had only existed outside this part of his life. And now, as she looked at the young European Princess taking all of Danyl's somewhat reluctant attention, she concluded that she would never be in this part of his life either.

She must have taken her leave of Hashid and Elizabeth, and must have bid appropriate farewells, and must have on some level taken in the stark beauty of the palace, the detailed tile work, the arches and mosaics left by previous generations of rulers, but could remember very little of it by the time she reached her 'rooms'.

Michaels had stopped just shy of becoming the bellboy, pointing towards the small holdall she had last seen on the plane, now positioned alone in the centre of a room that swamped it and made it seem tiny and out of place; an oddity in this incredible, regal set of rooms. Because it wasn't just one room. It was three.

A lounge, bedroom and the most stunning bathroom she'd ever encountered. The bath was…well, it was almost insulting to call it a bath. It was big enough to fit at least five people in it, and at a push she could probably have managed a half-decent 'lap' if she'd used breast-stroke.

And if this was the only taste of a life she might have known then she was going to take it. Before she said goodbye for the last time.

An hour later, her skin both slightly pink and shimmery with the incredible rose-scented oil she had allowed herself to use from the bath she just hadn't been able to resist, despite her shower only hours before on the plane, she stood wrapped in a towel, in front of a wardrobe that had literally stolen her sense of self.

These clothes were for her? There were so many. Did Danyl always keep a stack of clothes for women at the palace? Were there more rooms scattered around this wing, perhaps each room assigned by dress size?

She pressed her eyes closed against the sudden and unwelcome threat of tears. She knew she was good at putting a brave face on things, but, really. What was she doing here other than just torturing herself?

A knock on the door cut her free. It must be Danyl. She'd just tell him that she couldn't go through with it. That she would give him back his money, that she was sorry... She'd tell him anything at that point just to make it all go away.

She opened the door and it took her a moment to recognise the two beautiful and immaculately dressed women standing on the threshold of her rooms.

'Emma?' Mason asked, and the chestnut-haired woman broke into a smile.

'I wasn't sure if you'd recognise me. We've met, of course, but you always had...'

'A horse beside me?' Mason asked with a small laugh.

'Well, an entourage of stable hands and John standing steadfast beside you. This is Anna,' she said, bringing the other woman with her into the room. Anna was strikingly beautiful, with long dark hair and a stunning smile.

'So you're the one who tamed the Greek billionaire,' Mason said, and then suddenly felt awfully sure that this was not something one said to the wife of Dimitri Kyriakou.

'Yes, indeed I am,' she said with an unselfconscious

pride. 'Danyl sent us up here to see how you were getting on.'

Mason stood there in the towel and gestured to the wardrobe. 'I must admit to being a little more familiar with jodhpurs or jeans than empire waists and stilettos. I'd say that you've arrived not a moment too soon,' she said. 'I'm not ashamed by who I am and where I come from, though I'd rather not look like an Aussie outbacker tonight. Not sure that would go down so well with Queen Elizabeth.'

'Yours or Ter'harn's?' Emma asked, amused.

'Either,' Mason replied.

She was surprised by the easy camaraderie she felt with these two women, but realised it was who they were, as much as what they were here to do, that made it so. They were completely comfortable in their own skin, and there were no ulterior motives, no snide sideways assessment that she'd often encountered back in New York during her time there.

As they flicked through the array of incredible dresses Mason sent a prayer of thanks to Danyl for sending them to her. They distracted her from her fears and helped her get ready in a way that would allow her to fit in. Perhaps the evening wouldn't be so awful after all.

'That woman has been sent to torment me!' Danyl exclaimed over his glass of whisky.

'What—Mason? I thought you brought her here,' Antonio said, deliberately misunderstanding him.

'Amata,' Danyl practically growled.

'Are you surprised?' Dimitri asked. 'You sought out the most reputable matchmaker there is, then discarded every single prospective bride she sent your way. She does have a reputation to uphold and you're singlehand-edly destroying it.'

'She's not *that* bad, Danyl. She's just…'

'Young!' all three declared simultaneously.

'The poor girl has clearly only been sent here to make you play ball,' Antonio concluded.

'The poor girl has been decreed my last chance,' Danyl replied.

'I don't see why you are persisting with it,' Dimitri said of Danyl's attempts to find a bride. 'You'll find the right one, when you're ready.'

'Oh, don't be so smug. Just because you both have fallen in love, doesn't mean it's contagious and I'll sud-denly catch it. I don't need love. I need a queen,' Danyl said with alarming finality even to his own ears.

But even his harsh words couldn't wipe the smiles from his friends' faces, and Danyl couldn't quite bring himself to begrudge them their happiness. Each had been through their own torment, and each had come through it with a ring on his finger, and a beautiful woman on his arm. Women they loved.

And as if his chain of thought conjured them from mid-air, a knock came on the door to the study, and in walked three of the most beautiful women all three men had ever seen. It would have been a lie to say that it took Danyl a moment to recognise Mason. He knew her instantly, and the dress she was wearing, the way she looked…it stole his breath.

A shimmer of purple clung to her lithe form. It spar-kled every time she took a step, the entire length of the material covered in small purple crystal beads, making it look as if they clung to her skin rather than the barely-there material. His eyes ran up from her feet to where the material pulled across powerful legs, then a deliciously flat stomach, and up to where her perfect breasts were encased in more detailed beadwork. The low neckline clung over the slopes of her chest and his tongue stuck to the roof of his mouth. He'd always desired her, always known she was beautiful, but the purple against her sun-tanned skin was undoing him. Although then he looked a little more closely and saw a pale tinge to her cheeks, and something in her eyes that struck him hard.

Something was wrong.

He frowned, taking in Emma and Anna, who in direct contrast were almost giddy. Eyes bright, and each containing a happiness that was practically vibrating from them.

Dimitri let out a curse from beside him.

'Anna! You told them,' he accused.

'I couldn't help myself. And besides, everyone will start asking as soon as they realise I'm not drinking at the party tonight.'

Danyl's usually quick brain stuttered to a halt, but Antonio caught on much more quickly. Antonio pulled Dimitri into a bear hug.

'Another one? Already?' Antonio demanded of his friend.

Pregnant.

Anna was pregnant.

But, rather than congratulating the happy couple, all he could do was look at Mason, who was refusing to meet his eyes.

And once again it felt as if the bottom had fallen out of his world.

CHAPTER SIX

April, ten years ago

DANYL WAS NERVOUS as hell. He'd seen Mason race a hundred times in the last few months. She was incredible on the back of a horse. Glorious even. But this was the biggest meet she'd ridden in and there was a sense of tension in the air. Mason had garnered the attention of many of the big syndicates and quite a few of them were here today, like him, just to watch her. Her training had been nothing short of furious. Six days a week, morning and afternoon, if she wasn't with the horses she'd be in the gym, doing circuit training that would have cut even the fittest men down to size. By the time she collapsed on his sofa on the few days a week that she would stay with him, she would all but gaze dazedly at him while he ate his dinner. For some reason her training limited her to one—impressively large—meal a day.

Her dedication and determination put him to shame, and he'd used that. Somehow her drive had only ignited his. He'd always had good marks, but his tutors were beginning to see something else in his work. A creativity in his thinking that they congratulated themselves on unearthing. But it really didn't have anything to do with them. It was Mason. Talking to her about his thesis, his projects, he discovered that she had a different way of looking at things and he met her curiosity and built on it.

The only time she shied away from any conversation topic was when it concerned her mum. They'd skirted around the issue, and each time he could see the scars and hurts caused by her abandonment. Each time he'd tried to soothe away that pain, and even if in his deepest heart he didn't think his assurance, his affection, would ever be enough to fill the hole she'd left behind, it wouldn't stop him from trying.

He ignored the vibration of his phone. It would either be the palace or Antonio or Dimitri, and he could afford to give none his attention right now. He was in the private members' box, surrounded by his security detail, who were amusingly almost as concerned as he. Over the last few months, she had managed to wrap them all around her little finger.

His feelings for her had multiplied like a never-ending algebraic equation, increasing each day and each moment they spent together until it felt as if it would burst from his chest. He hadn't quite put them out there though. He didn't want to distract her, and he wanted to cherish this, these feelings.

A commotion began to build at the starting gate. They were about to bring the horses out.

Mason felt a little off. She couldn't describe it any other way. She was worried about Rebel. He didn't seem... And that was the problem. She just couldn't put her finger on it. She'd mentioned it to Harry and together they'd checked him over, hoof to ear, checked the paperwork recording all the feed times and care instructions. Nothing had changed since yesterday. Harry had looked at her and said that she'd be fine. Implying that she was transferring her concerns onto Rebel. She knew that wasn't it. This was what she loved. She lived for it. In the last couple of weeks she and Rebel had spent more time together than she and Danyl. She knew Rebel's moods, his likes, his dislikes. She could tell if she was riding him even with her eyes blindfolded. And she'd trust him even then. But...

They were being called to the starting gate, and she guided Rebel more with her legs than the bridle and leads. Her fingers were callused and cold in the April wind. Her legs, muscles, were tired but ready, almost relishing the burn that was to come.

Her heart began to pound, with fear, with anticipation, with hope. This was the beginning of the thrill of the win, to prove how good she was. The chance to prove to her father that the time he'd spent with her all those years growing up wasn't a waste. That the fact he'd chosen to stay, chosen to keep her—it was worth it. She wanted so desperately to see the pride in his eyes when she told him about her latest win. It was a drug she couldn't quit.

And Danyl. Somehow her need to impress, to succeed, had enveloped him too. He was there, always, distracting when she needed it, laughing and loving when she needed that. He was incredible and her feelings for him were compounded each day.

Rebel flicked his ears back and shook his head as they neared the other horses. Now wasn't a time for distraction, however. Now was the time for her and Rebel.

She leaned down and whispered calm, soothing words into his ear.

'It's okay, Reb, we'll just take this little road here and

be back in the stalls for sugar and oats in no time. We have great things ahead of us, love.'

He leant his head towards her mouth, shaking her out of his way, or leaning into her words; she'd take the latter. Her hand stroked over the smooth, powerful length of his neck, the way he liked it best. And she allowed herself to smile. This was what it was all about.

The commentator blared across the crowds below and the starting bell sounded before Danyl had quite prepared himself for it, his eyes taking a little time to catch up, so that they were almost into the first corner of the flat before he could pick her out. His hands were wrapped around the private box's white metal railing and in the back of his mind he felt that for the first time all his personal guard had their eyes on someone else: Mason. He'd seen her take Rebel out a lot of times when he'd been able to escape his studies and he couldn't quite shake the feeling that there was something slightly wrong, slightly off about the smoothness with which they usually rode together.

The furious pounding of horses' hooves and legs, the speed they were travelling at, rather than heightening his excitement, suddenly began to unnerve him. And, as if he could somehow sense the future, sense what was about to happen, he sucked in a lungful of sharp, cold air, just before it happened.

'And she's down. She's down. Rebel and rider are down.'

The scene in front of him was shocking in its brutality. He'd seen Rebel stumble, his head dipped, and the sudden drop in speed forced the other riders either out of the way or into the back of him. It was a pile-up of horse flesh and limbs, and while the race carried on Mason was somewhere at the bottom of it.

His throat hurt suddenly and he couldn't work out why, until one of his men jerked his arm and he realised that he'd been shouting. Screaming even. But he couldn't take his eyes off the carnage; he couldn't move until he'd seen her.

As the rest of the horses cleared the scene he saw Mason struggle to her feet as Rebel did the same. But the horse couldn't make it off the ground. People were rushing towards them from the edges of the fencing. She reached out to the horse, but Danyl was sure he could see the whites of Rebel's eyes from here.

He turned to exit the box, but one of his men stood in his way.

'You can't go out there,' the man said.

Fury roared to life; he felt it sting and scar his skin and his throat.

'Get out of my way.'

'No,' the man said, as he morphed into an immoveable mountain.

Danyl went to push him out of the way, but he dodged Danyl's arms.

'You can't go—it's too dangerous.'

'I don't care,' he said, trying to push past him, when an arm reached out to hold him. Danyl struggled against the restraining force, inflaming his anger. He struck out at the men, uncaring of his blows or where they landed, but his personal guard were too good. One wrapped his arms tight around Danyl's torso, and curses and shouts did nothing to remove the hold.

'I order you to let me go.'

Silence met his command, and finally he swung round

so that he could at least see back to the racecourse. An ambulance had appeared near the scene and he could see Mason arguing with someone, standing between the man and Rebel. He thought he saw Harry arrive and pull her gently out of the way. He was so distracted, focusing on Mason, that when he heard the shot his heart, his breath…it all stopped.

Mason collapsed and for a moment he thought that the bullet had struck her. All his senses focused on her, and he could have sworn he heard her cries. The sound cut through him like a knife and he all but collapsed in the arms of the men holding him back.

He struggled once more, ineffectually, desperate to reach her.

'You can see her later, just not now.'

'Dammit, get out of my way.'

'No, sir. This is for your own good. This is for the good of Ter'harn. You can't be seen with her just yet. And certainly not in this way.'

'She needs me! I am your boss—let me go.'

'No, you're not, sir. Not yet. Your father is.'

Danyl paced the length of the apartment. He'd spoken to Mason on the phone briefly while she was at the hospital being checked out. She had a fractured ulna, but aside from the damage to her forearm she was incredibly unharmed. But it wasn't her physical hurts that concerned him. She had been almost monosyllabic, and quite clearly still in shock. Devastated by the loss of Rebel, a horse she'd grown to love over the last few months.

Danyl had sent Michaels to retrieve her from the hospital, his treacherous head of security still preventing him from going to her, and he couldn't rest until he'd seen her.

Michaels opened the door to the apartment and Danyl rushed to where Mason hovered, her shoulders hunched, one arm holding the other, a white cast covering the wrist up to the elbow. She looked so small, as if she was trying to make herself even smaller, as if she was still reliving the fall from Rebel and protecting herself from invisible dangers.

He took her into his arms and she all but collapsed. Huge great sobs wracked her thin frame, and she shuddered and shook in his arms. He picked her up; the lightness of her body had once delighted him but now he only saw its vulnerabilities, its weakness.

He took her straight into the bathroom and put her on the seat while he started the taps running in the bath. He took her chin in his hand and gently lifted her gaze to his.

'They…they took blood samples.'

'I'm sure they just wanted to cover their bases with Rebel.'

'*My* blood samples.'

Danyl frowned.

Shock and confusion were setting in and she began to shake. He pressed a glass of red wine into her hands. If he'd had brandy he would have given her that, but she just shook her head and didn't stop. As if she was rejecting more than the wine, more than the pain and bruises he could see coming up in the spaces not hidden by her clothes.

He began slowly taking off one layer of clothing after another. This wasn't a seduction—this wasn't about physical desire. He managed to remove all of them, without Mason seeming to notice. The heat from the bath had filled the room but still she was shaking. Danyl guided her into the hot water, quickly removed his clothes and got in behind her, pulling her against him, wrapping his arms around her as if to protect her from what had already happened. Mason's tears fell from her face into the water in the bath, but they gently grew to a stop, along with the shakes that had rocked her body as if from the centre of her being.

As Danyl wrapped her in a dressing gown, after drying her, and led her to the bedroom, where he encouraged her to get into bed, his feelings began to swamp him. As he watched her close her eyes, and drift into a restless sleep, he felt his anger grow once more. Anger at how guilty he felt for not being there the moment he'd seen her fall, for not being able to protect her, for not being able to be 'seen' with her, as his head of security had ordered. And he promised himself in that moment that he'd *never* let his duty come between them again.

The sound of her mobile phone ringing drew Mason from her sleep. For a moment, she was confused. She was in Danyl's bed, but alone. Her hand reached out to the space where he'd slept, which was still warm from the heat of his body. She wanted to nestle into it. Draw from that heat.

Memories from the previous day crashed through her like a cascade, each accompanied by the sound of a gunshot. The moment she'd felt Rebel stumble, the way his head had drawn her down, the fear that formed before she'd even had a chance to figure out what was going on. The slam of the grass-covered ground vibrating through her body as she'd hit it. The searing pain in the forearm she'd put out to try to soften her fall, the snap of Rebel's bones, not hers, cutting into her like a knife. The sheer terror she'd seen in Rebel's eyes, as if he was so far gone as not to understand the greatest threat of the vet's gun. She'd known it was the right thing, she still knew that, but guilt, hurt, shock built in her chest now, as painful and mind-numbing as it had been yesterday.

Her phone hadn't stopped ringing. She flung out an arm, nearly knocking it from the bedside table, finally registering that the call was from Harry by his assigned ringtone.

'Are you okay?' His gravelly Southern voice sounded in the earpiece.

'Fractured ulna, eight weeks in a cast. What happened? Where are you?'

'I'm at the stables. Hold on.' His voice became muffled as he shouted words to someone else. 'Listen, Mason. I'm being investigated by the Racing Commission.'

'What? Why?'

'Rebel had painkillers in his system. And an anonymous accusation has been made against both of us. Apparently one of us dosed him up so that he could race.'

'But Rebel didn't have any injuries. There was no need for him to be on painkillers. And if he had been, then I wouldn't have run him.'

'I know. I know, and I wouldn't have either.'

'Why would I have drugged a horse? I'd never do that, Harry, I swear.'

The silence from the phone unnerved her.

'Harry?'

'They said *you* were on drugs too.'

Her mind scrambled to the hospital the day before. 'They took blood and urine samples from me yesterday.'

'I know.'

'You know? How?' she demanded.

'It's all over the papers. The Racing Commission have taken this very seriously.'

'Because I'm a woman?' she said furiously.

'Because whoever this anonymous source is has shared it with nearly every single newspaper in the country,' Harry growled.

'Okay,' Mason said while her brain scrambled. 'Fine, I've nothing to hide. I don't take drugs. But who could have dosed Rebel?'

Harry didn't have an answer to that and said his goodbyes before hanging up the phone.

Her head throbbed as she got up from the bed too quickly, the ache in her arm almost forgotten as she tried to see her way through how her life had changed so much in just twenty-four hours. She blocked out the images of Rebel in his last moments, broken, terrified, tortured, before the vet had done what needed to be done.

She made it to the bathroom before throwing up. Shaking, she brushed her teeth, showered and dressed to go and find Danyl. She needed him. She needed his warmth. But as she got to the slightly open bedroom door she heard the sounds of a hushed argument from the lounge.

'You have to extricate yourself from this.' It was a voice she didn't recognise, and one she took immediate dislike to. It was nasally and thin. 'The bad press surrounding the death of the horse, the accusations…it will do irreparable damage to your reputation.'

'I don't care. I'm staying here. I'm staying with Mason.'

'You should seriously consider returning to Ter'harn. Your parents want you back, and your classes are finished. You could submit your dissertation over email. You no longer need to be here.'

'What I need to do and where I need to be is here, Taruq. That's the end of the conversation.' Danyl's tone was increasing both in anger and volume.

'You have become infatuated with a silly little girl who wanted to play jockey and couldn't, so she drugged a horse, and that horse is now dead.'

The man's last word hung in silence, a silence that held her breath and heartbeat hostage. Horror crept across her skin, mixing with outrage and grief.

'Get out,' Danyl said. It was quiet, but no less terrifying for it. She imagined the battle of wills going on in the room next door—she could almost feel the intensity from here.

'I said…'

Apparently Danyl didn't need to finish the sentence. A commotion on the other side of the door happened and the horrible nasally man left without much further fuss.

But as he exited the building he left the door open to Mason's sudden realisation that he was right. That the bad press the man had alluded to would somehow taint Danyl. Taint them both. Irrevocably.

The door in front of her, not just the one in her mind, flew open and there he stood, instantly seizing on his own realisation that she had overheard if not the whole, at least some part of the conversation.

'How are you feeling?'

She looked up into his eyes, eyes that betrayed none of the conversation he'd just had. His whole focus was on her and it both soothed and ached at the same time. Could she really tie him to her now? She'd seen what the press could do to a jockey after the death of a horse. She understood it. It was an outrage. It was the dark side of the career that she loved so much. To take such a pure thing as racing a horse, and for it to be tainted by drugs and death... The ground swayed beneath her feet.

Danyl saw the moment the blood left her face and caught her just before she collapsed. He took her back to bed, and called out for someone to call a doctor, anyone, anything that could help right now. Mason waved off the offer of a doctor, and instead turned and buried her head back into the pillows. He stayed with her for an hour, comforting and soothing as she drifted in and out of sleep.

When he was sure that she was asleep for longer than a few minutes he went back out into the sitting room, where he found three of his men, all with faces grimmer than his own.

'Report.'

'There are investigators searching the stables. A few have been over to the room she shares with Francesca. She's been telling anyone who'll listen that Mason would never do anything to hurt either Rebel or herself. But the housing is surrounded by reporters. Whoever made that accusation made sure that this wasn't going to go away.'

'And the trainer? Couldn't he have drugged the horse?'

'All reports show that he's straight up, no priors, no need. He's good at what he does.'

Danyl rubbed his head in frustration.

He looked to Michaels, and he could see the concern etched into the older man's eyes. He'd been with the family since his father was at university, having been placed with him at Eton. 'She's okay, Michaels. She's strong,' he said, not quite believing it but hoping it.

'And the test results?'

'We'll have them by five p.m.'

Danyl gave a curt nod. 'I don't want to be disturbed for anything else.'

If he'd taken even one second before turning back to the bedroom, he would have seen determined nods acknowledging his request. But he didn't. He entered the bedroom, took off his clothes and climbed into bed beside Mason, pulling her sleeping form into an embrace. In her sleep she clung to him, while torturous dreams sent shivers and jerks through her delicate body.

Just after five in the afternoon, Mason woke at the sound of a knock on the door and became aware of Danyl dressing quickly and leaving. It took her a moment to focus; she desperately wanted to stay in bed, but her body had other ideas. Along with the aches and bruises that were gently humming beneath the surface of her skin, she was hungry. Her stomach let out a determined growl as if to make its complaint fully known. She peeled back the covers and gently swung her legs over the side of the bed. Deciding that she could make it the rest of the way, she pulled on a pair of leggings and grabbed a shirt from Danyl's wardrobe.

She entered the sitting room just as Danyl was closing the door on whoever had just been to see him. He looked about and, without his having to say anything, the two guards quickly slipped out of the room.

She frowned; it wasn't unusual for them to be either alone or with the men in the same room, but there was something heavy in the air. Something she couldn't quite understand.

'You should sit down,' Danyl said.

She looked at him, at the hundreds of emotions he was

trying to hide. Causing a chain reaction beneath the surface of her own skin.

'I think I'll stand,' she replied. She didn't know what was coming, but she was sure that it was better to meet it on two feet.

'The test results came back.'

'Oh. That was…quick.'

'I may have put some pressure on the tests being done as soon as possible.'

'Why? They're only going to come back clean. I've never taken drugs in my life,' Mason stated, still unsure as to what Danyl was hiding.

'Yes, your test results came back negative for any drugs in your system, and the Racing Commission are dropping any and all lines in that particular investigation.'

'But what about Harry? Are they dropping that?'

'I don't know. But that's…there's…'

'What?' Mason asked, shaking her head against the strange way he was behaving. She could see it. There was something else. Something that suddenly hooked impossible weights over the butterfly wings that had leapt into her stomach at the negative test results. 'What is it, Danyl?'

'The tests also showed that you're pregnant.'

CHAPTER SEVEN

December, present day

'WHEN DID YOU find out?' Mason heard Emma ask Anna
as the group made their way to the ballroom. She saw
nothing of the stunning architecture, nothing of the liv-
eried staff, heard nothing of the gentle sounds of a live
orchestra playing in the background, past the blood rushing in her ears or the ache blooming in her breast.

She *did* feel Danyl's gaze on her like a weight, chain-
ing her to the past where she didn't want to be. She tried
to shake it off, both Danyl and the past, and the hurt that
had been simmering beneath the surface ever since she'd
seen him at the camp in New South Wales, or even before that, the *years* before that.

Mason could be forgiven for thinking she'd stepped
into a fairy tale. Thousands of little lights covered the
ballroom walls, and candelabra glittered in the warm
air of hundreds of bodies swirling around the room in
conversation or dance. Uniformed staff were sweeping
around the room with silver trays containing champagne
flutes and canapés.

She cast a glance unconsciously to the exits, as if stor-
ing that information until the point at which she'd need to

use them. And she would need to use them, she realised. She would not last all night. Not now.

She spotted John standing in a corner looking out of place and dressed, both amusingly and uncomfortably, in a tux. She smiled, the sight of Antonio's old stable master, and later her trainer for the Hanley Cup, bringing back comfort and familiarity. She made her way over to him after an absentminded farewell to the Winner's Circle Syndicate and their partners.

'You don't scrub up too badly, John,' she said by way of greeting.

'Was about to say the same, McAulty.'

She liked that, even now dressed in clothes that had first taken her breath away, and then taken almost her identity away, he could still treat her the same way. They stood back from the crowd, clinging to the edges like wallflowers.

'The sheikh has put together an impressive shindig,' he said, clutching a champagne flute delicately in his meaty fingers, as if worried he might accidentally break it.

'Yup, but I'd settle for a beer over this lot,' she replied.

'Ha! Not sure I'd be able to get my hands on a half 'n' half over here. It's good to see you out and enjoying yourself.'

She nodded noncommittally. 'How's V? He make the journey okay?'

John nodded, equally noncommittally. 'The Queen's expecting some kind of show-and-tell.'

'We're all to troop out there and see him?'

'Yeah,' he relied grimly.

'He'll love that,' she replied, relishing the taste of sarcasm on her tongue, rather than pain.

'He'll handle it. But he'd be better for seeing you.'

'I've missed him,' Mason admitted.

'Reckon he's missed you too. V's okay with the lad they've got lined up to ride him for the New Year's Day race, but he hasn't taken to him the way he did with you. *And* Antonio's been complaining. He might have won the Hanley Cup, but he lost that horse to you.'

Mason smiled, guiltily pleased that Veranchetti hadn't bonded as well with his new rider. She silently promised herself that she'd go and find him later.

'How's your Da?' John asked, cutting through her thoughts.

'Not bad.'

'Good stock, that man.'

Yes, she agreed silently, he was, and an idea began to form. 'Have you thought much about what you're going to do now?'

'Well, with Antonio and Emma all set, I was thinking of going back home. But it's wet there. Not so great on the old bones.'

Mason shrugged a shoulder, knowing that the hard sell wasn't necessary. John made up his own mind about things. 'If you fancy something a little warmer, have you considered Australia? Dad would be happy to have you. If we survive the next few months, that is.'

'I've heard about the set-up you have there. Helping wayward kids. Sounds like a mighty fine project you've got going on.'

'It is,' she replied, her eyes shining with pride.

'No more races?'

'I don't think so. As mercenary as it sounds, I just needed the percentage of the purse.'

'Not mercenary. Just doing what you had to do. It's no easy thing, McAulty. But you did it.' And for a moment

Mason let the pride and respect in John's eyes wash over her, taking away some of the sting of the present with it. His gaze locked on to something over her shoulder and by the time Mason had looked to see the Queen descending on them and back, John had disappeared. Not mercenary. Just doing what he had to.

Danyl looked over the mop of blond curls that barely reached up to his shoulder, trying to form an exit strategy. This latest, and most definitely last, cruel punishment from Angelique was it. He knew he was being punished from the series of unsuccessful dates over the last eighteen months. Not that there had been *that* many international social functions that allowed for such get-togethers, and he wasn't desperate enough to be spotted by the press having an intimate dinner for two, where neither knew the other from Adam.

'And that was when I realised that my foot had caught the tablecloth and pulled all the plates, cutlery, glasses, the whole lot from the table into the Prime Minister's lap.' A light giggle that sounded rather close to clinking glass poked into his thoughts uncomfortably.

'That's great.'

'Great?' Amata replied uncertainly, and he realised he'd not heard a single word she'd said. He smiled apologetically, hoping to take some of the sting out of his latest social faux pas.

'Oh, the Prime Minister thought it was hilarious,' she replied, giving another little giggle. Something in her tone caught Danyl's attention, but when he looked at her she seemed just as bright-eyed and bubbly as she had since he'd first laid eyes on her.

'Amata, can I ask you something?'

'Of course,' she said serenely.

'I know why I'm using a matchmaking service, but you…?'

She smiled, her shining eyes clearing momentarily to reveal a surprising glimmer of sharp intelligence. 'I'm sure that I don't have to tell you of the price we pay for duty.'

'Is that what you're looking for? Someone who would understand that price?'

'There is understanding the price, and already having paid it. I believe that you are the latter. As I am.'

The sincerity in her words startled him, and for the first time since meeting her he believed that this was the only true thing Amata had said.

But the strange spell that had been cast about them was broken as his father came to meet them and Amata, rather abruptly, descended into an arpeggio of giggles, slapped him—surprisingly hard—on the arm, and told him off for being silly.

'I really am so pleased that you came,' said Queen Elizabeth—or Sheikha, or Her Majesty… Mason wasn't quite sure how to address Danyl's mother. 'It wouldn't have been the same without you,' she said, taking Mason's arm and tucking it into hers and starting to lead her around the outside of the ballroom.

Mason, as she had been from the first moment she had seen the handwritten invitation from the Queen, was a little bemused. She couldn't see why her presence in Ter'harn was so important. Nor could she quite fathom why she was suddenly feeling like a society miss, taking a turn around the room at her coming-out ball in Edwardian England.

'May I ask…?'

'Why it was so important to me for you to be here?' the older woman asked before smiling. 'My son inherited his interest in horses not only from his father but also from me. I used to love to ride, but after Danyl was born it became…' She shrugged. '*I* became a little more nervous. Motherhood gave me a beautiful son, but also a great sense of my own mortality. That and, though I was a good rider, I did not have your considerable skill. I am also aware that the press has not always been kind to women riders—you in particular. I wanted to counter that somewhat in my own small way.'

There was so much in that simple declaration that Mason struggled to unpick all the threads, but above all she was touched at the determined support from Danyl's mother. Touched, envious and slightly grieved that she had missed that kind of maternal support so easily offered by the Queen of Ter'harn.

'It's quite something to get your head around, isn't it? All this royal stuff,' Elizabeth said with a delicate gesture of her hand, encompassing not only the room, the guests, but also so much more.

'This royal stuff?' Mason repeated, surprised by the inelegant way of referring to the spectacular gala the Queen, by all accounts, had singlehandedly organised.

'It took me quite some time to get used to it.' As if realising that Mason wasn't quite keeping up with the thread of the conversation. 'Becoming a royal,' she clarified. 'Hashid had to do a lot of convincing to make me think that this could work. *I wasn't always a princess,*' she confided, sotto voce.

Mason smiled. She was beginning to warm to the dramatic patters of the older royal woman.

'I did a *little bit* of acting,' Elizabeth said in such a way that Mason was to realise she was no mere bit-part actress. Mason didn't need Wikipedia to know that she had been the star.

'Hashid saw me in a film, said he fell in love at first sight and tracked me down to America. Oh, I knew the moment I set eyes on him, that was it. But I made him work for it. It's not good to let men think they can have their way easily.'

A tinkle of laughter, light but really quite loud, drew their attention across the ballroom, producing a rather tired and indulgent groan from the woman beside her.

'I wish Danyl didn't feel the need to go to such extreme lengths to avoid…well. Whatever it is he's avoiding. But I have to say I really don't know what that matchmaker of his was thinking with this one.'

'Matchmaker?'

'Ter'harn tradition dictates that before the sheikh can pass the country's rule on to his son, that son should be married. Horribly patriarchal, I know, but marriage was seen to herald the birth of an heir that would continue the rightful rule for future generations and admittedly it has worked for Ter'harn. We have done much to counter some of the more…outdated traditions, but Danyl still feels the need to adhere to this one. And as we're not getting any younger, he's stepped up his efforts to find the perfect bride.'

Mason couldn't help it. Snippets of conversation from the past were pulled into the present. In New York he'd struggled with it, she knew. He'd felt the heavy weight of the far-off crown and had uncomfortably accepted it. But no matter how she tried, she couldn't fit the passion-ate, exuberant sincerity she had known of Danyl with the cold, calculation of a matchmaking service to find his Queen.

'He hasn't always been like this. I know that he comes across as harsh and demanding…but once, a long time ago, he used to laugh. Ah, he had a perfect laugh.' Mason looked up at the Queen, and was surprised to find her eyes glistening with a sheen of what looked suspiciously like tears. In that moment, Mason too saw the filter of who Danyl had been, and who he appeared to be now. And in that moment Mason found herself wondering if the Queen might actually know more than she was letting on, might even know what had caused that change.

'Got to say, Danyl, she's looking stunning tonight.'

'Who? My mother?' he asked, slightly outraged.

'Mason,' Antonio replied, barging his shoulder against Danyl's. 'Though your mother is looking beautiful as always,' Antonio hastily added.

'Dimitri, it really is great news. Congratulations,' Danyl said, forcing out the words he should have spoken hours ago.

'Yeah, well, as I only found out this morning, it's still sinking in. It seems Anna just couldn't keep it to herself. I'm really looking forward to it,' he said somewhat bashfully. 'I missed out on so much the first time round.'

Danyl was surprised to find no trace of anger in Dimitri's words. Once it would have been something to behold. Antonio frowned at something over his shoulder, and Danyl turned to see Sheikh Odir Farouk making his way towards them.

'Welcome to Ter'harn, Your Highness.'

'Thank you for having me, *Your Highness*,' Odir replied with an easy smile.

'Allow me to introduce you to Dimitri Kyriakou and Antonio Arcuri. Antonio, Danyl, this is Sheikh Odir Farouk.'

'The famed Winners' Circle, feared by every racing syndicate throughout the world,' Odir replied, just a gentle trace of humour hanging on his words. 'Thank you for inviting me. Your mother has outdone herself, yet again.'

'Yes, she has,' Danyl agreed, quickly scanning the room to find her, and more than a little unsettled to see her talking with Mason. He turned back to Odir. 'Is your lovely wife here?'

'Somewhere,' he replied, unconcerned. 'She's probably on the phone to the nanny, worrying about our children.' Odir gestured to Danyl, stepping away from Antonio and Dimitri a little. Danyl followed and watched as Odir reached into his tux and produced an envelope. 'Malik asked me to give this to you. He said he'd got what you wanted, and to say if you need anything further you only have to ask. He didn't seem to like the subject of the investigation very much and was almost gleeful at the opportunity to do something about it. But I managed to talk him down. The rest is up to you.'

The envelope felt heavy in Danyl's hand as he thanked Odir and turned to a secluded corner to scan the contents. Although it wasn't necessarily a surprise, he felt outrage and fury and something like regret. But perhaps with this, Mason might be able to finally put the past behind her. Perhaps he could finally put the past behind *him* and move on. Because in truth, that was what he needed to do. Move on.

He looked up to see Mason leaving through the open

French windows that led out into the gardens. Good. What they had to say to each other did not need an audience.

Mason sucked in a deep, hopefully calming breath of cool air, letting it soothe her heated skin. There was no way that Danyl would have told his mother. Mason certainly hadn't told her father. He'd known that something had happened in New York. Perhaps something more than Rebel's death. But she'd never spoken of it. Not to him. She wasn't stupid, and had known that she needed to talk to someone. A few years after she had returned to Australia, one of the councillors at the farm had noticed that something was wrong and had offered to talk to her about it. And she had. And it had helped. A little.

A noise behind her startled her, even as her body recognised the tangible effect of Danyl's presence. She'd always known him—even when she couldn't see him. The hairs on her arms would lift, there would be a tingling sensation at the nape of her neck…even ten years hadn't seemed to be able to dull that awareness.

The white of his shirt stood out like a beacon in the darkness. His gaze was hooded by shadows and that powerful brow of his. He'd undone the bow tie, the black silk material dangling from his neck, the shirt open at the collar. He looked…incredible. He always had. Desire stung her cheeks, and chest, need bleeding out of her in response.

He held out a Manila envelope to her, but something told her that she didn't want to take it.

'What is it?'

'Read it.'

'I'm not sure I want to.' Mason still hadn't taken the envelope.

'It was Scott.'

'What?' Confusion coursed through her veins.

'Scott drugged Rebel, told the press and the Racing Commission it was Harry, accused you of being on drugs. He was the one who caused Rebel's death. Not you. And sadly Rebel wasn't the only horse to die as a result of his machinations.'

'Scott?' She couldn't quite believe it, though if she was honest, perhaps she could. She hadn't given him a second thought after that race, after the discovery of the test results and after what happened next.

'Perhaps if you read it yourself, you wouldn't have to parrot back everything I say.'

'I don't want to read it.' And suddenly she was angry. She was angry at him for not letting it go. For digging into a past she wanted left alone. For making her come here...for everything. 'What is this supposed to be, Danyl? Some fix-all for the pains of the past?'

'It's supposed to be the truth. Finally. The press can leave you alone, you can race again if you want to. Other syndicates will certainly take you on now.'

'And you think that dragging it all up again will make it better? *I* knew that I was innocent, that Harry was innocent. I don't need some piece of paper to prove it.'

'No, but the press do. And if you want them off your back, then this is the way.'

'This? The only thing this is, is the ability to finally stop Scott from hurting other horses, and other jockeys. Yes, this should be known. It should be known by the authorities. But this isn't for me.'

'I thought this would...'

'I don't want you digging around in my past, Danyl.'
She was almost shouting now.

'Don't you mean *our* past?' he bit back.

'No! I mean mine. For all intents and purposes no
one knew you were there. You weren't mentioned in the
press, you weren't involved. So no. *My* past is where
you've been digging and I want you to leave it alone.
Leave *me* alone.'

Mason turned to walk away, but Danyl's fingers
wrapped around her forearm and brought her spinning
back round and almost smacking straight into his chest.
She had to look up at him, craning her neck back just to
see his face.

'But it's not just your past, is it? It's mine too.' Danyl's
voice was rough and scratchy. Not from desire, or need,
but hurt and pain. 'And you're cutting me out of it, just
like you did last time. We can't avoid this any more. We
have to face this so we can move on.'

'Is that what you want? To move on? With a practically
perfect queen who will want nothing from you, demand
nothing more of you? Tell me, Danyl, why on earth did
you hire a matchmaker?'

'Who told you that?' he demanded roughly.

'Your mother. She seems very well informed.'

'It is none of your business.'

'But you're allowed to meddle in mine?'

'I am when it stops you from doing what you want to
do with your life.'

'Did you ever stop to think that maybe I was? That
I'm happy working on the farm with kids that need help?'

'No. I don't think you're happy, because I know what
you look like when you're happy, Mason.'

'And what about you, Danyl? What is it that you want?'

'I want free of this!' he shouted, no longer able to hold back all the emotions she provoked in him. 'This hold you have over me. You think it's easy for me? You being here? Look at you!'

'What, dressed up like some wannabe princess? Is the rugged Aussie girl showing through a little too much?' The bitterness in her voice threw petrol on the flames of his anger.

'No, dammit, beautiful! You're beautiful!' For about a second everything was quiet, as if she was as shocked as he that he'd finally said it. 'Every time I look at you it hurts, because I know how you taste, I know how you feel under my skin, I know how your eyes darken when you climax, and I know the sound of my name on your lips when you do is like nothing else in this world.'

They were trembling now. Both of them. He'd never spoken to her like this before, with this raw passion that seemed to frighten them both. Ten years ago their relationship had held an innocence, a sweetness, but this… This was like nothing he could have expected or imagined.

She was about to run again. He could tell. He could see it in her eyes. But he couldn't just let her go. Not this time.

His hand released its grip on her upper arm and moved to her neck, anchoring her in place. His lips crashed against the softness of hers, punishing and powerful. Hard against soft, heat against cool. He thought—feared—for a moment she had turned to stone. But a second before he was about to pull away her mouth opened and his tongue danced with hers. Need like a firestorm swept through his body, blocking out all thought, all awareness other than that of her.

Fireworks tingled over his skin, beneath his clothes, flames scorched his neck as her arms swept up around it, clinging to him with the same desperation he felt.

It wasn't enough. The kiss just wasn't enough.

He drew her against his chest, relishing the feel of her soft breasts against the hard muscles there. His hands swept down over the sides of her body, his thumbs reaching to outline the curves of her breasts. Her gasp fell into his mouth as she must have felt his hands, gasps, sighs, but it still wasn't enough.

He reached to her thigh, pulling behind her knee, bringing it up to wrap around his hip, pressing his aroused length against her core, and relished the way her body sank into his. They had fitted together perfectly. Something he'd marvelled at ten years before, and still now today.

He pressed open-mouthed kisses down the side of her neck, leaning her back into his arms in an embrace that left her chest exposed to his lips. Her skin tasted exactly the same—honey and warmth and that taste of her that was unique.

It was pain and pleasure all mixed together.

His hand pulled up the skirt of her dress. He needed to feel her skin, needed to know this was real and not the fevered imagining that had distracted him even when she was a million miles and ten years away from him. The thin material covered in thousands of crystals poured over the fine wool of the tuxedo jacket, and his hand met the silk of her skin, pushing up her impossibly thin ankle, over the smooth length of her shin, up to the strong, muscled thigh and round to her backside, pulling her towards him, pressing her against the strength of his arousal. It was enough to nearly undo him right there.

He jerked his head back in shock. How had he forgotten? The gala, the palace, the past…

CHAPTER EIGHT

May, ten years ago

'ARE YOU SURE you want to do this?'

'Yes.'

'Really?'

'I don't see any other option.'

'It may be a sacrifice you should not make. It would leave you...vulnerable. Exposed.'

'I've thought through the consequences. It is a risk I'm willing to take.'

'So be it. Make your move.'

Mason picked up the figure of the Queen and moved it across the chessboard to take his Bishop. Without pause, Danyl took her Queen with his Castle decisively. Mason allowed a small smile to play with the edges of her mouth. She might be learning at chess, but she'd never win at poker.

'What?' Danyl asked, noticing.

She allowed him a moment, to take in the chessboard, to realise his mistake, before moving her Knight into checkmate.

'And the student becomes the master,' Danyl said without malice or anger, only pleasure at seeing her win.

He swept her up onto his lap and peppered kisses across her face and neck, before Mason pulled away to lock eyes with him.

'Are you sure you don't mind?'

'Mind about what? You beating me at chess? Yes,' he said, finding that spot beneath her ear that never failed to drive her wild. 'I mind greatly,' he said, his words slightly muffled. 'I might,' he said, pulling back to look at her, 'have to have you eliminated. I can do that, you know. I'm a prince.'

The sheer arrogance in his voice reduced her to giggles. Something Mason found was happening with alarming frequency these days. Before her train of thought brought back the seriousness in her eyes.

'I'm not talking about that… I mean the baby. I know we don't…'

'I'm ecstatic. Over the moon. Ridiculously happy,' he said sincerely. His eyes had sparkled the moment he'd told her about the pregnancy. The moment they realised they were going to have a beautiful baby. 'And I can't wait to tell the world!' he half shouted into the empty apartment.

She stifled her laughter again. 'What about the press…?' she asked, doubts and hurt still present behind their shared joy.

'The drug tests were negative and the press knows it. I'm sure Harry will be cleared too. And there's nothing that time won't heal. Nothing. Mason, I'm… I'm humbled by what we're about to embark on. I couldn't imagine anyone else I'd rather be with, or do this with.'

His hand swept around her middle. And in that moment she knew that he was feeling the same as she, that neither could quite believe that they had created a child.

He placed a kiss over their joined hands, gently replaced her on the sofa and disappeared off to the kitchen.

The last month had passed in a whirlwind. Danyl had arranged for a doctor to come to the apartment and visit before he'd even told her the news. It hadn't upset her, which surprised her—it only made her love him all the more. He'd been concerned about the effects from the fall, but the doctor had reassured them that both mother and child were healthy and strong. She'd been worried about the painkillers she'd been taking, but the doctor switched her to paracetamol, which she'd used sparingly since then. Her arm was still in a cast, but that would be off within the month.

When she was with Danyl, she couldn't contain all the joy she felt. It was as if there was a burst of light emanating from her and she never felt the need to try to stop the beams from falling wherever she went.

But... And there was a but. When he had to leave for college, or for the diplomatic duties he'd assumed at the embassy recently, she was left in the empty apartment and doubts began to creep in. What if he was only with her because of the baby? What would happen once the baby was born? How would she handle being the wife of the King of a country she'd never seen?

But even further beneath all of those were the ones about being a mother, were the ones about her own mother.

Danyl poured Mason her new favourite hot drink and went to the office to Skype his parents.

Mason took the cup, allowing the heat to seep into the palms of her hands, and went to stand beside the window. She'd wished on more occasions than one that there was a balcony, wished she could feel the air on her skin the way she did back home, in Australia.

Now that she had felt the stirrings of motherhood, now that she was about to embark on it with Danyl, it made her even more aware of the feelings she'd spent the best part of twenty years pushing aside, pushing down away from her consciousness. The sliver of pain she'd allowed herself to feel at her mother's abandonment now felt like a river she wasn't sure she could stop, building in speed and force every day she got further into the pregnancy.

Individual thoughts about it seemed almost intangible, but the one thing, the one word that rose above the rest on the tide, was *why*? Had it been her father? Had it been her? Had she not been enough? Had her mother not loved her enough?

Whether it was hormones, or just plain emotions, she couldn't tell. It didn't really matter, she supposed. She hadn't been enough to make her mother want to stay. And now that fear was beginning to bleed into her relationship with Danyl.

Was she enough to make him stay, or was it just their child that had bound them together now? What would have happened had she not become pregnant? Would that horrible man have managed to convince Danyl that she wasn't worth it? She knew those thoughts were harmful, knew she wanted to clear her mind, worried somehow that the negativity she sometimes felt would affect their baby. But every now and then the tide of questions and thoughts snuck up on her and swept her off her feet.

Danyl had noticed. She realised that. Every now and then he would look at her when this happened, and would find a way to distract her. Pull her back to bed, challenge her to a game of chess she was fast learning to master, offer to cook her some food—something that usually ended in disaster. For a man who was soon to rule a country, it had surprised her that he couldn't even make toast without burning it, let alone the coffee he liked so much.

That she let him distract her, without telling him what was going on in her mind, was perhaps a little worrying. But when he looked at her with that twinkle in his eye, the one that said they shared the most amazing secret of all time, she couldn't resist. She fell willingly back into this bubble of joy they had created almost forty storeys above Central Park in New York.

Danyl closed down the Skype conversation with his parents. It was killing him not to be able to tell them about Mason. He might not have wanted to immediately take up his royal duties back in Ter'harn, but he loved his parents, and had never once kept a secret from them. He could already imagine his mother's reaction. The surprise, the joy that she'd feel. Almost the same way he felt when he'd first realised that Mason was pregnant. He'd heard about other men in the same position as he, feeling unsure, worrying about the future. He'd felt none of that. He'd simply known that it was right. So right. It was as if some alien sensation had swept across his skin, sinking deep into his bones and somehow changing his DNA, in a way that made him feel complete. Made him feel a thread of happiness and focus that he'd never felt before.

For the first time in years he'd felt able to see himself taking up the reins of responsibility from his parents. Slowly easing himself into life in Ter'harn, learning everything he could from his father so as to best be able to continue the amazing work he'd done. And all of this would happen with Mason by his side.

He didn't think for one minute that it would be easy for her to find her royal feet, but she was intelligent, a fast learner, kind and more compassionate than he could have imagined. She would make an amazing queen. One who didn't hold back from challenging him, or his thoughts, to ensure that he really was seeing the right way through his thinking. He thought back to the comments he'd received from his professors at college. Each and every one of them had remarked on his renewed vigour as he attacked each paper, each project with relish.

Danyl knew that he was excited, that he was wrapping up his time in New York so that he could take Mason back to Ter'harn with him. That would, of course, only be after a stop in Australia to visit Mason's father. Ideally it would be better to tell his parents and her father together, but that would have been not only a logistical nightmare but also simply impossible. There was no way he could get his parents to fly to Australia without first telling them what was going on. Eventually they'd agreed to wait until the cast was off her arm and she'd been given the all-clear before they flew out to her father and then on to his parents.

He was nervous about meeting Mason's father. But he also couldn't wait. Danyl wanted to tell Mason's father just how much he loved her, how much he wanted to take care of her, and just how much he wanted to marry her.

He walked back into the sitting room to find Mason looking out of the large floor-to-ceiling windows, and paused. He sometimes found her here, almost tucked behind the curtain, as if afraid to stand fully in front of it. He wasn't sure if it was because she felt safer in the shadows, or if it was the shadows that drew her. But he was reluctant to intrude on those thoughts. He'd tried once, and she'd avoided telling him what was on her mind. And ever since then, it felt as if it was something private, something she didn't want him to see.

'Mason?'

'I've been thinking,' she replied without looking at him. He never knew what she would say when she was like this. It could be anything from dinner plans to a scathing critique of his latest college essay. Anything and all of it was welcome as it cut through the silence that covered her like a shawl.

'Mmm?' he prompted, walking over to her, lending her his warmth and strength as he pulled her back against his chest.

'What do you think of the name Faaris?'

'Faaris as in…?'

She turned, and a small smile pulled at her lips, but her eyes were bright and shining.

'As in *knight*… I think. Translation apps aren't always—'

'It's perfect,' Danyl replied, prising his tongue from the roof of his mouth. 'It also means *hero*,' he added. The name had taken him by surprise, but it probably shouldn't have. 'You think we're having a boy?'

'I think we're having a football player, whatever the gender,' she said, laughing and rubbing her stomach.

'You've felt the baby kick?'

'No, silly. It's too early. But I've definitely felt something. Perhaps just the warm-up, but—'

He stopped her words with a passionate kiss. One that took them all the way into the bedroom, for a *very* long time.

Mason woke in the middle of the night and nearly cried out. The sharp cut of pain low in her belly was unbearable. She reached out to Danyl, who woke immediately.

She knew the grip on his arm was strong, but the moment his eyes locked on to hers she saw the terror that she felt reflected in him, before another wave of pain crashed through her body. If she cried out, she couldn't tell, but Danyl was suddenly a blur of activity. He grabbed his phone, and for a moment she couldn't quite understand what he was doing. The words he shouted into the phone were unintelligible beyond the pain, the fear. Her hands were at her stomach, her whole body curling in on itself as if to try and contain, trying to protect.

The taste of fear stung her throat and tongue. Bitter, acidic. She was trembling now, tears falling freely down her cheeks. No, no, no. It was a mantra in her mind, tumbling out into the dark bedroom of the apartment.

She shook her head against the thought, as if that would stop whatever was happening. She refused to give it voice, refused to think it, superstition and desperation warring in her breast.

Danyl picked her up and carried her through the apartment, into the lift and down into a car in the underground car park, faces and figures surrounding them all a blur. She buried her head into Danyl's shoulder, refusing to let her mind stop on a single thought, wanting to block out everything, the pain, thoughts, the past and the future. She couldn't let her mind rest on a single thought, because if she did…

Danyl's soothing words of reassurance disappeared into the night, carried away on the air as blurred lights faded in and out of her mind while the car swept through the dark, empty streets. It was as if they were the only people in the whole world and she clung to his shirt in desperation as yet another wave of pain took away hope, took away a future she had only just let herself believe was possible.

* * *

Mason closed her eyes against the bright white lights of the room around her. She never wanted to open them again. Perhaps if she didn't, it wouldn't be real. It would all go away. Monitors beeped into the silky, numbing co-coon that had descended over her mind. It would all go away. She just needed it all to go away.

People were talking in the corner of the room and she just wanted them to shut up. Anger, fury, grief was a heady concoction sticking to her skin, to her arms, to her body, hurting and fighting in her chest, her heart. A heart that felt as if it had been irrevocably damaged. As if nothing would ever be the same again. A sob racked her body, tears that should have been exhausted by now fell from her closed eyes, down her cheeks, and she didn't have the energy or the desire to wipe them away.

The smell of disinfectant, of cleaning products, dripped into her stomach, nausea not far behind. She curled in on herself once again, her hands going to her womb, where the tiny flutter of life that she'd once held on to so strongly wasn't there any more. She tried to bite back the moan that came from the deepest part of her heart, she tried to contain it, not to let it loose, but she couldn't.

She wanted to scream. To shout, to cry, to fight, but the fight was already over. She knew, in some distant, rational part of her mind, that she needed to stop, that there were things she needed to do. But she couldn't.

There was nothing left now. Nothing in her belly and nothing between her and Danyl, other than a grief she could barely even begin to allow herself to feel.

The noise in the background stopped, a door opened and closed, and she felt a dip in the bed beside her.

Danyl's smell wrapped around her, just as his arms did, pulling her back into his chest. And she let go.

Danyl pulled her against his body in the back of the limousine. He hadn't been able to stop doing that since she'd woken in the middle of the night. It was as if he needed her there, pressed against him, felt that perhaps she needed it too. He felt the tremors through his body as if they were his own. If he was honest, they could have been. He just couldn't get his head round it. It was impossible. He shook his head against the words the doctor had spoken, and stopped. He didn't want to wake Mason, who had seemed barely able to open her eyes as they walked from the hospital room out to the waiting car. She'd been inconsolable. He'd not really given much thought to that word before. But now he knew. Truly, he knew what it meant. Grief, loss, helplessness—it all ate away at him, taking pieces of the future he thought he'd have and eventually reducing it to nothing.

Guilt. Guilt was the hardest one. How had he failed to protect Mason, how had he failed to protect his child?

The doctors and nurses had given them phone numbers and details of grief counsellors and groups. Little pieces of paper pressed into his hands. Paper instead of...

His mind shielded itself.

They made it to the lift, up to the apartment and through the door into a place that screamed at them of a future that they no longer had. They'd made plans here, they'd made a future here, they'd made and lost a baby here, and it was all too much.

'Let's go. We can stay at a hotel for a while,' he decided.

As if he hadn't even spoken, Mason left his side and

walked slowly over to the chessboard. Sinking down to the sofa, she reached out to the present she'd given him and clutched it in her hands. The little Knight piece, completely different from the rest of the set.

The piece with the name of the child they would have had.

His heart too full of unnameable emotions, Danyl's quick mind went to practicalities. Perhaps they should go away for a while. Somewhere new, somewhere to regather themselves. They could be on a jet within the hour, taking them far away from here. But, looking at Mason, he just didn't know if that was what she wanted.

He felt helpless. So helpless. And it scared him, cut him deep.

Since leaving the hospital he had tried to provide comfort, tried to talk, but she had retreated into a shell, unable or unwilling to communicate. And he understood, he felt the pull to do the same. He wanted to curl in on himself, but he couldn't. He needed to be strong. For her. For himself.

Danyl hadn't realised that he was pacing. It was only when Mason looked up at him, and he saw the change in her face, the determination in her eyes, that he felt the stirrings of something he'd wanted to reject, avoid, deny ever since they'd left the hospital.

'Let's go away,' he said, forestalling the words Mason was struggling with. He knew what they would be. He knew they would hurt, they would damage and wreak a havoc he just wasn't willing to face. 'We can go to…' he said, searching for a place she might have always wanted to go to and realised he wouldn't have been able to name it. They hadn't spoken about such things. It had all happened so fast. But he'd been okay with that. He knew. He knew because he loved her, and he knew she was about to…

'No.'

Mason could almost hear his mind whirring. She became aware of an ache in the palm of her hand and when she opened it she was half surprised to find the small stone figure of the Knight indented on her skin.

She wanted to be alone, but she also wanted him wrapped around her and to never leave. She wanted to pretend that the last few hours had never happened. That they were still within a bubble where all thought, all sanity had somehow been excluded. She'd lost her child, her job…what on earth did she have to offer Danyl now apart from grief?

All those childish fantasies of going to Ter'harn and marrying the Prince…the silly fears of whether she would fit in, whether she would be able to be his Queen… They all now just seemed foolish and impossible. Her cheeks flamed with grief and pain as she remembered the words his senior advisor had uttered in this room.

'You have become infatuated with a silly little girl who wanted to play jockey and couldn't, so she drugged a horse, and that horse is now…'

Her mind shied away from the word, stumbling over and falling to the hard ground. There was a rational part of her that knew she wasn't ready to make decisions, that knew she wasn't ready for anything other than sleep that would numb her mind and take her far away from the waking nightmare of the day. But if she didn't do this now, she might never have the strength to do it.

Her mother had walked away from her and her father when she was a child. But could Mason honestly say that she'd be happy to tie Danyl to her in the absence of one? Soldering their lives together with a silver seam of grief was surely an even worse reason to stay together.

'We could go anywhere in the world. Let's just—'

'No. Danyl, it's time we saw this for—'

'Don't finish that sentence. I don't want to argue with you.'

'I'm not arguing with you. I'm telling you. There's no need for you to be bound to me any longer. I'm not...' She struggled to force the words out, knowing the pain they would cause, knowing that they would cast their future in stone. 'I'm not carrying your child any longer.'

'Mason, please—'

'Let's face it,' Mason said, desperately searching for all the reasons they shouldn't be together, 'this was only ever a fling that got out of hand. I could never be your wife! Look at me. Even your advisors think so.'

Mason couldn't even look him in the eye. Each excuse, each word, though somehow right, was like ash on her tongue. How could something be both truth and lie at the same time? His body was shadowed by the light of the sun creeping over Central Park. A new day arriving to erase the last four months...

Danyl had yet to say anything, but he was practically vibrating with emotions, emotions coming right at her, clashing with the ones already swirling inside her.

When he did speak, it nearly broke her.

'Please don't do this. Please. Give us some time. We shouldn't be making any decisions right now.'

'There's no point, Danyl. I'm... I'm going to go back home to Australia for a bit,' Mason said, realising the truth of her needs. She hadn't thought it once, but the moment she said it she knew it was where she needed to be.

It might be killing her to walk away, but she was one person. Danyl had a whole country ahead of him to look after. And he couldn't do that with her beside him, a constant reminder of grief and loss. It would shape everything, and she'd be left trailing in his wake, never knowing if he was still with her because of his love, or because of his guilt. She knew, because that was how she felt. Grief was turning and changing their entire relationship, painting it in swathes of dark colours already.

'Please, Danyl. You have to go. You have to let me go.'

CHAPTER NINE

December, present day

'No,' HE SAID, the word pressed against her lips, the word he should have uttered years before.

He pulled back, looking down at Mason, her eyes shining with confusion as bright as any star in the Ter'harn night sky above them. And then, reading her thoughts, he watched her belief that he'd meant 'no' to the kiss enter her eyes and she turned away. She scanned the garden around them, as if looking for witnesses or escape, he wasn't sure which.

'We're not doing this any more.'

'No, of course not,' she said, pulling out of his embrace, her fingers flying to her mouth as if to brush away, or seal in the kiss they'd shared, he couldn't be sure. But one thing he did know was that she had completely misunderstood him.

He shook his head, as the sudden realisation and renewed determination had shocked him to the point of speechlessness. Instead, he grabbed her wrist and started leading her through the palace gardens.

'Where are we going?' she called to him, jogging to keep up with his determined strides.

'Somewhere we can finally talk.'

* * *

Mason could still taste him on her tongue, feel him on her lips and skin, his firm hands moulding the length of her leg, the feel of him pressed against her core… Her body was wracked with tiny little tremors, but that was nothing compared to her heart.

Somewhere we can finally talk.

Danyl's words repeated in her mind on a loop, and she started to pull back against the hold he had on her wrist, her body doing what her mouth couldn't. She realised she was shaking her head.

'Danyl, don't. I can't…'

'You walked away from me once, Mason. I'm not letting it happen again. Not until we've dealt with the past. Haven't you felt it?' He stopped short, turned and she almost ran into his chest again. *'Haven't you felt it?* That anchor pulling you back, making it almost impossible to move forward?' He looked at her intently, as if trying to see if she felt what he did, and Mason was terrified of what he *would* see there in her eyes. Of course she had, she wanted to scream. How on earth were they supposed to move on? she wanted to know. Even after all these years. He gave a short, sharp nod, and resumed his march around the outside of the palace.

With his free hand he plucked his phone from his pocket and barked unintelligible orders into the mouthpiece. All the while Mason's mind and chest were a swirl of fear and confusion, guilt and grief. Didn't he realise that she'd walked away to protect him? That she'd done what she needed to that night so that he could have a life, a future that wasn't lost in pain and grief?

And if there was a small voice reminding her gently

that she'd also done it to protect herself, she refused to acknowledge it.

They arrived at a tarmacked circle, on which sat a small, sleek, black-as-night helicopter. A man in a jumpsuit moved from beside it, only the glowing high-vis stripes across the suit allowing Mason to pick him out in the dark.

He ran to Danyl, said a few words, cast one look at Mason, clearly too well trained to allow any signs of surprise, and left.

'What's going on? What are we…?' Danyl had ignored her, and instead pulled her still by her wrist up to the open door to the helicopter.

'Get in,' he commanded.

'Danyl!'

'Get in,' he repeated, his tone as dark as the night around him, and Mason knew that there'd be no arguing now.

There had been glimpses of this autocratic persona when she'd known him ten years ago, but it had always been softened by an almost amused, self-aware arrogance. The Danyl she'd seen presented in the papers, on the day she'd first met the Winners' Circle, and at the race meets ever since…*this* Danyl…was a different beast altogether. Once again guilt rose, poked and prodded. *You did this*, her internal beating stick whispered to her. *You did this to him.*

He guided her to the handle at the roof of the helicopter and she pulled herself into the seat. She might have managed it with more dignity in a pair of jeans and flat boots, but heels and a crystal-lined dress made it slightly more difficult. She could feel Danyl restrain the urge to just push her into the seat from her backside.

He slammed the door behind her, walked around the front and got into the pilot's seat.

'You…you fly?' she said, her voice expressing the disbelief she felt to her core.

'Of course. I'm a prince.' The sentence said so many times ten years before was now void of all that had made it a shared joke between them.

He gestured for her to put on the headset as he began flicking at buttons, checking the various monitors around the small cockpit, if it was even called a cockpit in a helicopter—Mason honestly had no idea. She automatically ducked slightly in her seat when the rotor blades started up above her.

Within minutes they were jerking up off the ground, up, up and up. With her stomach left about fifty feet below them, Mason's hands gripped the armrests of the seat, her knuckles white. It took another ten minutes for her to begin to relax, unable and unwilling to speak to Danyl in case she distracted him. She could no longer tell if the air between them was vibrating with tension, frustration or just the engine of the helicopter.

Loosening the grip she had on the armrests, and prising her eyes open, she began to look out of the smooth curved windows. She couldn't help the gasp that fell from her lips as she looked out across the night-covered country. Little dots of lights, gathered like sequinned silk, outlined small towns and villages. With the palace behind them, she could just make out the thick velvet blanket of the sea in the distance. No light penetrated there, and for a second she wondered if Danyl would just take them out there and keep going.

She was surprised to see a stretch of mountains far off to the left, and it reminded her of home. Her gaze stuck to them as if she could draw from them the peace that she usually only felt in the Hudson Valley, until she felt the little helicopter dip.

Beneath her Mason could see the lights of the helicopter pad, guiding Danyl down to a surprisingly gentle landing. She waited in the seat for Danyl to say something, but as soon as the chopper was switched off he ripped his headset off, got out and was at her door before she'd even moved to remove her own headset.

She expected him to pull open her door and yank her out of the seat, but instead he seemed to check himself, waiting for her to be ready. Mason took a breath and released the handle, his hand waiting, hovering mid-air to help her disembark. She took it with some trepidation, hating that she knew he would notice her trembling fingers.

She stepped down onto the tarmac and looked up into his eyes, seeing nothing of their surroundings. She saw pain, pushed deep down, but she saw it. Pain, yearning, and so much else that matched what she was feeling in her own heart. She wanted to raise her hand to his cheek, to soften it all somehow, but he turned away, leading her off the helipad and towards a set of stone stairs.

As she followed him down the stairway, she looked up and stopped in her tracks. It was a fairy-tale castle, hewn from the rocks on which it sat, as if it had been formed by them, rather than perched on them. There were several layers of gardens, and pathways, decreasing in size, leading up to the main body of the castle. It reminded her of a sentinel looking out to sea, keeping a constant vigil against incursion from the ocean. It was simply incredible.

'What is this?' she asked, a surprisingly warm wind whipping her words back and forth.

'The Summer Palace,' he replied, paused, just as she was, on the steps, as if taking it in for the first time. But still his gaze refused to meet hers.

Danyl pushed onwards, and soon they were walking through the large entrance foyer, just a few staff waiting to greet them. Orders were issued, people disappeared, and he pulled her onwards through the large stately rooms she didn't have time to really look at, and out onto a balcony area, if you could call the broad expanse she found herself on a balcony. He'd finally let her hand drop and it was only when she was bereft of it that she realised the warmth his touch had provided.

Danyl watched Mason walk over to the stone balcony overlooking the Arabian Sea. It was a sight that stole his breath, but it wasn't the ocean he was looking at. The lights from the large state room behind them picked out the crystals on Mason's dress, purple shimmers cascading down her back and legs every time she moved, each one striking him like lightning.

He'd known it would come to this. Somewhere, deep down, he'd known. Perhaps that was why he'd fought so hard against Mason coming to the gala in the first place. But, for his mother, he'd done everything he possibly could to get her there, and now she was here. *Here*. Where he'd wanted to bring her all those years ago.

'It's beautiful,' she said finally, turning to him.

'Yes,' he stated, not feeling the need to add anything further. Not yet anyway. 'I wanted to bring you here to show you something.'

Confusion marred her delicate brow. But she, too, said nothing further. As if they each felt that words were too precious to waste.

He pulled his lips into what he hoped was an encouraging smile, rather than a grimace, and he held out his hand to hers. This time she would come of her own volition, he decided, refusing to drag her in his wake like a Neanderthal as he had done the moment they'd broken the kiss.

That kiss.

He'd had no control over himself. She had whipped up a spell that pulled him to her and he'd felt helpless to resist. And it was the first time in years that he'd felt peace. His hand stretched out between them, desperate to reform something of that connection, something of that peace. He would take what he could get right now, especially for where they were going.

Her hand, slightly cold in his, lay on his fingers, and he led her down the stairs at the end of the large balcony. He would have found their way to their destination, even without the small inbuilt solar-powered lights illuminating the path before them.

Over the years since they'd been in Manhattan he'd taken this route a thousand times. He'd never shared it with anyone else and only he had the key to the private garden. Not even his parents. It struck him now that they'd never asked him about it. It was his sanctuary, his privacy, and they'd allowed him that.

He led her to a circular wall of English-style red bricks, markedly different from the rest of the Moorish castle. Beside a small wooden door was an old stone bench, the seat and arms covered in a sweet-smelling herb.

Whether he was buying time before they entered the garden, Danyl wasn't quite sure. All he knew was that he needed a moment to gather his thoughts. To get them to the conversation they needed to have.

He sat heavily on the soft green herb-covered stone seat, looking up at Mason.

'Take a seat?'

'I...' She paused, as if sitting beside him was a fate she'd rather avoid. 'I'll ruin the dress,' she said with a shrug of her delicate shoulder. He'd have thought it was an excuse, if he didn't know her well enough that she *would* think of damaging the expensive dress.

He shrugged out of his tux jacket, laid it beside him over the moss-green living seat and gently tugged her down beside him. Next to each other, they each looked out over the rest of the gardens surrounding the summer palace.

Words escaped Mason. They flitted through her mind, back and forth, swept up in an emotional storm, failing to snag and catch, failing to land where she could bring them out into the open. She'd felt like this when she'd sought out the counsellor on the farm. She'd known that she needed to talk about it, to open up her grief, but the words had become clogged in her heart and chest. She'd tried so hard to stop blaming herself. That had been the work of the best part of two years. Wondering if she'd done something wrong, if the fall had caused it, if *she'd* caused the terrible loss of their child.

Consciously and practically, she knew that it was highly possible it had not been anything she'd done. Consciously. But her deepest fears would sometimes run free, waking her in the middle of the night—terrible pain and fear wracking her body with tremors—her body knowing enough to feel pain and loss, but her mind taking a second to catch up. To remember. And then would follow the avalanche of guilt—how could she have forgotten, how could she have to struggle to remember?—drenching her with ice-cold sweat and tears.

With each passing day, month and finally year, her grief had become a thread woven into her very being, the fabric of who she was. But it was a secret thread, invisible to the naked eye, known only to her...and to Danyl.

Unconsciously, her fingers picked at the skirts of the beautiful dress, and she almost started when she felt Danyl's hands lie over hers to stop them. She stole a glance at his profile, looking out to the public gardens and the palace before them. His jaw was clenched as tightly as the knot in her stomach.

'We need to...to talk about it. Because, Mason, I really can't move on until we do. I've tried, I really have, but seeing you again...when you approached us in that club...' The unspoken accusation lay heavily between them. *Why did you do it? Why did you come back?*

'I had no choice,' she said into the warm night air about them, shifting her hand in his. 'We were going to lose the farm and you were the only people who might be insane enough to take a risk on a jockey who hadn't ridden internationally in almost ten years. Especially with my reputation.'

'A reputation that will now be cleared.'

Mason allowed herself to take that in. Even though it was unlikely that anyone would care, all these years later, she felt...vindicated. Harry would be cleared too. He'd struggled for a while after Rebel's death, but through hard work and with head down he'd managed to rebuild his stables and reputation. But her? She'd hidden in the Hunter River Valley. She'd hidden from the world where she thought she'd be safe from prying eyes. But she hadn't been safe from the past.

'What will happen to Scott, do you think?' she asked Danyl.

He drew in a breath. 'I've passed the information on to the Racing Commission, who will probably look into it. The police may even want to investigate, though defamation is a civil matter, purposefully harming the horses... That could be criminal.'

Mason sighed, a little of the hurt leaving her chest. 'I'd not really thought of it like that. I... I was...'

'We weren't the only ones who could have uncovered him. Just the first. And *we* were a little preoccupied at the time.'

'But those first months...'

'*That* is what I was talking about. We were...happy,' he said, so sadly that it cut her to the quick.

'We were naïve,' she retorted, then regretted it. It had been an automatic response built from years of self-defence.

'Do you really feel that way?' Danyl asked, turning to her as if to try and read the truth from her.

'In a way,' she said, looking down at their hands, entwined. 'Sometimes,' she said, fighting the tears that rose unbidden to the backs of her eyes, 'sometimes it doesn't feel real. I remember the snatches of happiness, and think...we could never have been *that* happy. It couldn't have *really* felt like that. Because how can a person live like that? Feeling that constant level of...? They'd explode, wouldn't they?' She turned to him. 'And then I think that maybe it *was* like that. But only because it...' She searched for the words. 'It was like candyfloss. Impossibly sweet, so very delicate and ephemeral. It could never have lasted because there was nothing deeper, no solid layer beneath to support it.'

* * *

A wound Danyl thought had healed opened up in his chest. Not the one that covered his grief over their child, but the one that contained all the memories of his short time with Mason, the one where he'd buried his love for her, and cemented over the top. That same love was thrashing around in the bottom of the well, begging, shouting to be let out, crying to be heard.

'Don't do that,' he said, hoping she didn't hear the begging tone in his voice. 'Don't undermine what we had. You know it was more than that.'

'Really? And how would I know that? We were children, Danyl. So young, and so naïve. As if to think that we could meet, fall in love and live happily ever after.'

Fury ripped through him as her words tore apart their past. 'The only thing that stopped us was you leaving.'

'How could I stay?' she demanded, as angry as he felt. 'Our grief—'

'*Our* grief? Ours?' he all but spat. 'You held your grief as if it was your own. As if you were the only one who had the right to it. You left me and I couldn't share my grief, or provide you with comfort. I couldn't do anything.'

'I left because it was too much!' Danyl caught the silvery trail of tears tipping over her cheeks. 'I couldn't open up the way I felt, I couldn't open up those gates, because I was afraid that once they were open I'd never be able to close them again.'

'Perhaps they shouldn't have to be closed.'

'Closed or open, we couldn't have stayed together bound solely by grief. Grief instead of love. We were so young. I had my career and you had—no, *have* a country.'

The same powerlessness he had felt all those years

ago rushed over him, his thoughts, his skin, pulling at the hairs on his arms. He'd felt so lost. Supposedly able to protect a country, but not his child, and not the woman he loved.

'We lost a child,' Danyl said, turning to her, desperately wanting her to see, to feel what he was trying to say.

'We didn't lose him, Danyl.' Her words held the ache of grief and hot anger. 'He isn't waiting somewhere for us to find him! He died, and there's nothing we can do about it.'

'Nothing...?' he asked. 'I don't think that,' he said, rising from the bench. His fingers reached to the chain he wore around his neck at all times—the chain that held the key to the gate in front of him. He pushed open the old wooden door, framed by winter roses, and held out his hand once more for her to take.

Mason wasn't sure she wanted to see behind the door, but she knew that if she didn't she'd always wonder. Always want to know. She placed trembling fingers in his palm and drew strength from the warmth of his skin.

She stepped into the large round garden and stopped. Everything stopped.

Her breath, her heart... Tall eucalyptus trees stood proudly around the circular centre, the musty smell of mint and honey seeping into her pores and soothing the aches and hurts of her heart. Wild winter roses covered the stone walls, adding little bursts of colour to the tangle of greens and brick-red that met her.

In the centre of the garden stood a tall, head-height statue of a knight. The chess piece that had brought them together, that would have been the name of their little boy. The detail of the stone carving was so real, so lifelike. She walked towards it, her feet on a stone pathway that Danyl must have taken many times over the years. She reached up to the long face of the horse, her hands cupping its firm stone cheek as if it were alive. Her soft fingers grazed the roughly hewn stone, dancing over the details in wonder.

She took a sudden breath, an inward reflection of a sob, and greedily tasted the eucalyptus scent on her tongue. Eucalyptus and a large stone knight. Part him, part her.

'We can remember him,' Danyl said quietly. 'We can honour him by talking about him. By loving him still. But not by ignoring our pain and letting our grief outweigh our love. I loved him. You loved him. And he's here with us every day and to deny that, to make it dark and painful, undermines that.'

'You did all this?' she asked.

'It was the first thing I did when I came back to Ter'harn from America. I needed to…have something with me, somewhere I could go to, to remember him. To remember you.'

It was a beautiful, magical place. Vines and winter roses grew around the worn stone knight. The sun's first rays were just beginning to poke their fingers over the horizon, painting the small garden in beautiful soft yellows, the flowers just beginning to open under its touch. Perhaps Danyl was right. What if, in all this time, she'd only swallowed her grief, stifled her love? Her love for their child, and her love for him?

'When did you get so wise?' she asked, tentatively tasting the soft mockery on her tongue.

'I've always been wise, Mason.'

She smiled softly at the return of his…no, not arrogance. Self-assurance. Wasn't that what she'd first loved so much about him?

'But you never gave me the chance to share this with you. You retreated. You left me.'

His softly spoken accusation hurt, knowing that it was more painful because he was right.

'I couldn't… I couldn't open those gates, I couldn't share my feelings, because I thought if I did, if I said them out loud, I'd never be able to stop. That the grief was so overwhelming, I thought it might never end. It was too much, too soon and too powerful,' she finished, wondering if she was still talking about her grief, or had somehow begun to talk of her love for him.

'He would have been beautiful,' Mason said, looking up at the statue.

'He was.'

'But he should never have been the reason we were together.'

'He wasn't,' Danyl said. 'Not for me.'

The tears ran freely then, cascading from her cheeks, plunging into the dress and sparkling amongst the crystal beads. Each tear a regret, a sorrow, a hurt. Each one leaving her allowing her grief to morph into love, to recognise and embrace her feelings for their son. Danyl's arms wrapped around her then, holding her while she cried. Doing the very thing she'd refused to allow herself all those years ago. To allow him to provide comfort, support and love… To find peace with the man who had once stolen her heart, the man who had now given it back to her.

CHAPTER TEN

December, present day

DANYL LED MASON through the quiet halls of the Summer Palace, something fiery burning in his lungs. He'd thought that speaking with Mason, sharing their grief and talking of the past would help. He'd thought he'd finally be rid of this…this… He searched his usually eloquent mind for a word that would cover all the emotions, all the physical feelings of what he was experiencing.

Wordlessly he showed Mason to a bathroom in the royal suites. Leaving her there and returning to the lounge, he crossed the large open-plan lounge to the bar and poured himself a whisky, damning the early hour of the day.

Usually this was *his* time, the time he felt he owned, rather than the hours that duty chipped away at, that responsibilities stole. But, as the sun's early-morning rays reached out to touch the sandstone walls of the palace, it failed to calm him as it usually did.

She had cried. And for a moment he'd feared, just as she'd predicted, that she might not stop. For the first time since deciding to pursue this goal, this final resolution over the past, he'd wondered if he'd made the greatest mistake of his life. Her grief had struck against the walls he'd built around his heart, had made a mockery of his own. The tears she had shed before him shamed the ones he could only give alone.

He bit back the curse that clogged his throat. He was a fool.

Noticing the grip he had on the glass, he placed it carefully back on the bar instead of hurling it against the wall as he wanted to. A mirthless laugh escaped his lips. Yes. He was a fool to think that opening up the hurt and the pain would somehow allow him his freedom. And for the first time he allowed a voice he hadn't heard for years to suggest that perhaps he would never be free of Mason McAulty. That perhaps he didn't want to be.

The door to the bathroom opened behind him and, coward that he was, he couldn't turn, *wouldn't* turn to look at her. Her high-heels clipped across the marble flooring, counting down the moments until she reached him. Anticipation raised the hairs on his arms, exposed to her presence now that he'd rolled back the Egyptian cotton cuffs of his shirtsleeves. Somehow he sensed a shiver run through her delicate body. As if the warmth he'd felt at his back had been cut with ice. Had he imagined the soft twinkling of crystal beads shimmering together over the soft tremors of her skin? Did she feel it too? That arc of sensation that had survived all these years? That invisible thread that bound them together?

He'd flinched. She'd seen it the same moment a shiver ran through her body. Staring at the breadth of his back, shadowed by the sun's morning rays, she'd wanted to reach out to him. To feel the strength of him wrapped around her. The memorial he'd taken her to in the palace gardens had left her vulnerable, exposed. And, where once she'd hated that feeling, she knew he'd been right. Opening up her grief to them both had been cathartic. It had let both love and grief mix together, and find a way through the darkness into the light.

But Danyl had been wrong if he'd hoped that it would resolve the tension between them. Because now Mason felt it all. As if letting go of the hurts and embracing the love had somehow made her want him, need him even more.

It had always been there, she realised. From that first moment their eyes had met across the grand room in the Langsford. A burst of attraction that had rained down star-lights of need over them both. That was what sent the shiver across her skin now, that was what made her want to throw caution to the past, the present and the future.

A storm of need was building between them, a thing so powerful it was almost tangible. She raised her hand, feeling it against her palm, on the tips of her fingers. Danyl span round and caught her wrist, preventing her from reaching him. Her hand, hovering between them, inches above his heart.

'Don't,' he commanded. The word cut through the haze of desire built so strongly between them only he could undo it. But she could tell that his usually ironclad control was fraying under the same weight of need and passion she felt. She could see it in the gold flecks that framed irises rounded with desire, feel it in the way he was yet to release her hand, taste it as the faint, familiar sweet scent of whisky fanned out over her.

'I want this night,' she said, surprised that her voice held none of the trembling her heart experienced.

'You're in no position to ask for anything, Mason. You were the one who left, you were the one who turned away.'

And she resisted the urge to do so again, the dark tones in his voice a warning as much as a castigation.

'I had to. Can't you see?'

And that was the worst of it for Danyl, because he *could* see. It had been self-protection. And had he not been protecting himself all these years? Wasn't that why he'd embarked on the ridiculous search for the perfect, un-emotionally engaged royal union?

'But I'm here now,' she whispered. A promise, an offering.

'And for how long this time?' he demanded.

But she didn't need to answer. He could see it written in her eyes, across her face, and feel it in the pulse that flickered beneath his fingers still wrapped around her wrist. Her breathing was shallow, little puffs against his lips, and it wasn't enough. He needed the feel of her against him, needed the touch of her fingers, the cries of her pleasure.

She was offering him a way to exorcise their demons once and for all. She was offering herself to him. And he wasn't strong enough to resist.

He pulled her against his chest, unable to fight his need, his desire, himself any more. The moment his lips crashed against hers he feared that it might never be enough. Her lips opened beneath his tongue, allowing entrance to the soft, sweet promise of her mouth. Her free hand flew to his face, fingers threading through the dark swirls of his hair, pulling her to him, anchoring them together.

The crystal beads of her dress scratched against the cotton of his shirt through to his chest. A friction almost unbearable, but necessary. He pulled again on the hand he still held, relishing the feel of her chest against his, relishing the control he was barely able to leash. But as soon as he'd had the thought, he realised how wrong he'd been.

Mason walked him back to the chair in the corner of the room, her strength once again surprising him. The fingers of his free hand ran over an arm more toned and defined than the last time they'd touched. He wanted to feel more of her. Her legs, her thighs, the exquisite wet heat of her wrapped around him. He wanted it all.

Mason pushed him back into the chair, his legs bending the moment they hit the seat. Leaning over him, reluctant to break the kiss, she freed her hand from his grasp and grasped the heavy hem of her crystal-covered dress, pulling it up to her thighs, allowing her to place her knees either side of his legs as she lowered herself onto his lap.

For a heartbeat she wanted to lay her head on his shoulder, just to stay there, just to luxuriate in his strength, in his warmth. God, how she'd missed this.

But then his hands came around her hips, pulling her core deeply against the hard ridge of his arousal. The thin silken panties she wore met the wool of his trousers, but they might as well have been the emperor's new clothes for what little protection they gave against the onslaught of their mutual desire.

The feel of his hardened length beneath her was incredible, familiar yet heartbreakingly new. She wanted to give them this. She wanted them both to have this moment, this last time so that when they parted ways, when they finally said goodbye, it would be the thing they remembered. A last act of love they both desperately needed and deserved.

His fingers threaded their way beneath her dress, the tightness of the body stopping the pathway his hands were following at her hips. His thumbs came round the top of her thighs and teased the edges of where she so desperately wanted him.

He held her there, teasing, taunting, commanding her body with a touch. He pulled back in the chair, breaking the torment of his punishing kiss, and she knew what he wanted. She felt the same thing. He wanted to see the need in her eyes, wanted to see the sparks of the intense feelings sweeping over her, the edges of hysteria that would make her beg. Make her plead. She knew because she wanted that of him too.

Oh, God, it had never been like this. Ten years before it had been innocent, and playful. Now it was an intoxicating drug that she needed both more of and needed to quit. One last hit—that was how she'd come to think of this. But all thoughts fled as his thumb dipped lower, deeper, between her legs, running over the scrap of ashamedly damp silk covering her. She sucked in a breath, unable to hide the effects he was wringing from her. She cursed as his other hand slipped behind her, pulling her against him even more. He slipped a finger beneath the back of her thong, bringing the silk firmly against her clitoris, and she cried out loud, only the crush of his lips, the power of his tongue in her mouth closing off the wanton sound.

Without warning incredible waves of ecstasy pounded through her body, pulsing within her and rippling shivers across her skin. Her body, as if trying to protect itself from the punishing tide of the most powerful orgasm she'd ever felt, wanted to curl in on itself, but strong, powerful hands held her in place.

'I want to see it. I want to see you,' he growled into the space between them, unconsciously echoing the words he'd said all those years ago.

His hands left her then to seize at the material covering her body. He tore at the dress, ripping it at the seams, casting the shreds of both the dress and her only protection against him to the floor. Naked in all but the shoes and betraying silk scrap useless against her modesty, she was bare to him. His hands swept over her thighs and arms. With one arm encasing her, he gently pushed her back, his lips finding the curves of her breasts with unerring accuracy. He took her hardened nipple into his mouth and reignited the storm inside her. Her undoing so complete, she let her head fall back and simply indulged in the sensations he rained down over her.

Danyl couldn't get enough of her, taste or feel enough of her. He pressed hot, open-mouthed kisses down her neck and across her chest, over the perfect swell of her breasts, the faint traces of coconut and salt, the body scrub she still used, tantalising his taste buds. His fingers flexed against her arms as slowly the tremors of her orgasm sank into her skin. It was like coming home after too long an absence. It was both familiar and welcoming, but strangely discordant and unsettling. So instead of heeding the warning echoing in the back of his mind, he pushed on, making her body his home once again.

His lips found hers as his palms found her shoulders and he cursed. He wanted to feel her naked against his own skin, but he was still fully clothed. As if she'd come to the same conclusion at the same time, her quick hands flew to the buttons on his shirt. He went to help, but laughed when she batted his hands away without breaking the kiss. Mason pushed his shirt from his shoulders and ran her hands over his chest and back, sending shivers through them both. The need was so great between them it was almost too much to bear. He grasped her to him and stood, enjoying the small squeak of shock that fell into his mouth. He held her there with one hand, her legs around his hips, moving only to let his other hand rid himself of his trousers and underwear. He kicked off his shoes, toed off his socks and stepped towards the bedroom.

'No,' Mason said, shaking her head.

His breath caught in his chest.

He would stop. If he had to, he would. It might kill him, but he'd never…

'Back to the chair,' she commanded, and the impish light in her eyes was enough to soothe his fears.

He sat back down in the leather chair and relished the feel of her warm, silken skin against his. The smooth, strong muscles of her thighs swept over his and she giggled as the hair tickled the backs of her legs. Her knees came either side of his hips and she settled against the hard, hot evidence of his need.

'This is not a laughing matter,' he growled to Mason, trying to stop the smile forming at his lips.

'On the contrary, Your Highness. I've found it the only sure way to manage you.'

'I will not be managed by you or anyone else.'

'No? How about a bit of "careful handling", then?'

Her hand slipped between them and he caught her wrist. There was no way he could let her touch him. His body had been on fire since they entered the room and he would not shame himself like a green schoolboy. Their eyes locked in a battle of wills and he used the moment to move her into his hands, holding her above his lap, realisation dawning just before he brought her down on his erection and he plunged into the warm, wet heat of her.

Everything stopped. He could do nothing more than rest his head against her neck, her hands in his hair, holding him. Her breath shuddered out of her lungs, sending cascades of tremors through his own body. She was wrapped around him and he was buried deep within her, the two of them connected more powerfully than he could have ever imagined. But slowly his desire became impatient, restless. He moved his hips and Mason threw her head back, her knees locked against his hips, and he allowed her to set a rhythm that drew need and want from them both.

Soon the room was littered with the sounds of pleasure, the air as hot with them as he was. And he feared that he'd never be able to satisfy this hunger he had for her. A hunger that was nothing about his own needs, but all about hers. He wanted to hear his name on her lips, he wanted it imprinted on her skin, on her heart. As she was on his.

Soon all coherent thought was overwhelmed by the need to reach the impossible pinnacle she was driving them towards, his hips rising up to meet her, thrusting into her again and again and again, and still it wasn't enough. A fire lit beneath them reached up to cover his skin, flushed with need and want and desire, reaching over and into his chest, seizing him in a heady grip, and, as he found his release just as she did, buried deep within her, his last thought was that he could never let her go again.

* * *

It was the sound of the shower that drew Mason from her sleep. Refusing to open her eyes, she reached out to the smooth silk sheets of the bed Danyl had taken them to. They were cold. Her eyes flew open and she looked at the ornate clock beside the bed. She frowned, unable to tell if it was three in the afternoon or morning. A beam of sunlight filtering through the curtains confirmed her suspicions and she pushed herself up, relishing the unfamiliar aches in her body.

Her fingers went to lips bruised by kisses, her chin slightly sensitive from the shimmer of stubble that had swept over every single inch of her skin. A blush of shame and desire painted her cheeks at her wanton behaviour from earlier. It had never been like that ten years before. Sweetness and light, she supposed, had no place between them now. But as she looked around the empty room unease crept into her heart and she felt...alone and unsure. What would happen now? How would this change things? she wondered. *Would* it even change things? She heard the shower stop, and after a moment a door closed, but there was no sign of Danyl.

Frowning, she gathered up the silk sheet around her and made her way to the bathroom, peering round the door, hoping to find him there, hoping to find him gone.

It was empty. There was another door leading off the bathroom. One he must have used. She looked about the room, one wall full of antique glass, and she walked towards it, taking herself in.

Her hair was tousled and teased, her lips pink and plump, but it was her eyes that stopped her. Shining and bright in a way she hadn't seen since...since before...

She let the sheet fall into a silken puddle at her feet

and stood naked before the mirror. Little red marks of passion coloured parts of her pale skin, and she ran her fingers over them, tracing the path his lips and hands had taken the night before.

This is my body. Toned from hard work on the ranch, she'd never given much thought to its appearance. And she now wondered what Danyl saw when he looked at her. Was she just the uncouth jockey he'd had a dalliance with all those years ago? No. She couldn't lie to herself. The reverence, the true passion he'd shown her last night had changed something between them. Last night he'd set her grief free by showing her how to embrace her love instead of fighting it. But could she say the same of her feelings for Danyl?

She turned away from her reflection in the mirror, unsure as to what she'd see in her own eyes, and stepped into the most luxurious shower she'd ever seen. She relished the feeling of the hot water pummelling her skin, the soft, rose-scented bath gel smoothing over her body carelessly erasing the impressions Danyl had left there, and for a moment she regretted it. Regretted losing the scent of him, the feel of him.

She knew she couldn't hide in the shower for ever, but the warmth, the steam enveloped her in safety and she was reluctant to leave. Outside was unknown, what happened next intangible. But here, she was in that halfway house of the past, the present and the future.

Her conscious mind forced herself to turn off the water and she grabbed one of the towels—slightly rough, the way she remembered Danyl liking them.

Entering the bedroom, she realised that she had no clothes. Danyl had torn the fabric of her dress in his passion. Guiltily she peeked into his wardrobe, finding a pair of jeans, a belt and a white shirt that might just about work.

Cinching the loose denim with the leather belt around her waist and tucking the shirt in at the back, she went in search of her shoes. For some inexplicable reason, she felt she needed them. A form of armour against the day. She found them near the chair and slipped her feet into them, catching the sight of her reflection in the windows. She looked oddly 'on trend', as Francesca would have once said.

She stiffened as she saw Danyl behind her in the shimmery image of the window.

'We should return to Aram.'

She held back the words on the tip of her tongue. She'd been about to thank him. Thank him for making her confront the past, thank him for the magical time he'd given her, thank him for making her, even for just a few hours, feel as if she belonged to him again. But then the image of her standing there, the Princess of an empty castle, looking out to the wide-open sea, shattered all words and questions…shattered her heart.

CHAPTER ELEVEN

December, present day

HE'D MADE A MISTAKE. A monumental error in judgement. He'd thought that they'd talk and resolve whatever anchors were tying him to the past. He thought that sleeping with her would get her out of his system once and for all. He'd wanted to reset the past and to be able to move on with his life. But Danyl had been wrong. Instead, he had simply ignited an all-consuming need that fought in his breast, scratching and clawing to get out and hold Mason to him for ever.

He forced himself to concentrate on the small helicopter bucking and swaying in the wind from the sea, and not on Mason's small, quiet frame in the seat beside him. She seemed too lost in her own thoughts to fear the effect the weather could have on the chopper and for that he was partly thankful. Only when he set it delicately down on the helipad back at the palace in Aram did he allow himself to expel the breath he'd been holding for the last twenty minutes. He bought himself a little time, double-checking all the equipment, waiting for the blades to slow and releasing himself from the safety harness.

He turned, having finally summoned the courage to

say…something to her, but Mason ducked out of the helicopter and picked her way across the tarmac in last night's fancy heels and his shirt and jeans. He shifted his shoulders, imagining the feel of his clothes against her skin as she felt them. Instead a waft of shower gel rose up as if to remind him that her scent was no longer on his body.

He watched the gentle sway of her legs, accentuated by the heels, as she made her way to the aide waiting for her. He couldn't even imagine how she thought herself a rough Aussie outbacker. Even when they'd first met she'd had a natural grace, a little like the powerful horses she was able to command with a flex of her thighs. And there were more similarities than just their gait. She reminded him of a frightened thoroughbred. All tense muscles and wide eyes, waiting for danger, shaking off any attempts to touch or hold her. The hurt that she held to herself went deeper than the loss of their child, Danyl realised. And in that moment he knew that she'd never be his, never truly his, until they'd reached that deep, deep pain. And, although he hated the idea of opening that wound, he would. Because he needed to. Because she needed him to do it. Because, when it came down to it, Danyl loved her. He'd never stopped loving her. Not once in all these years.

She'd disappeared into the warren of buildings that formed the palace, and he had to stop himself from running flat out after her. His aide fell into step beside him as if realising the futility of trying to stop him.

'Sir, there are just a few things—'

'Not now.'

'But, sir—'

'I said, not now.'

Danyl saw Mason draw to a halt in the distance as if
struck still by the jarring sight of the party still in full
swing in the palace gardens. His mother had clearly organised an oddly English game of croquet while other
guests were grouped around tables dotted with drinks
and canapés. He picked out the figures of Dimitri and
Antonio and their partners, just as his mother clearly
picked out the sudden reappearance of Mason. He heard
his mother's soft, warm welcome and watched as she
beckoned Mason into the fold of people gathered about
her.

His quick mind making mental calculations of what
needed to be done, he knew that, as much as he wanted
to make his way over to his friends, there was a bigger
issue he needed to tackle. And a high-pitched feminine
laugh told him where he needed to go.

In Danyl's jeans and shirt, Mason felt horribly self-con-
scious, fearing that perhaps Danyl's mother would somehow just know that she was wearing her son's clothes,
that she would have somehow divined what had passed
between her son and the Australian jockey. But if she
had Elizabeth showed no signs of it. Instead the older
woman pressed a glass of ice-cool lemonade into one of
Mason's hands and a small quiche into the other, with a
look that told her not to argue.

It was then that Mason realised she'd not eaten for
quite some time, and without tasting a bit of it she swallowed down both the drink and the food. After satiating
her body's needs, she turned to take in the gathering and
her eyes were drawn to Danyl, as they always were. He
was standing with the young Princess. They looked good
together. The small, pretty blonde and the swarthy, tall,

dark and handsome man. Oh, Mason knew that the girl wasn't right for Danyl, and that he certainly wasn't in love with the Princess and in all likelihood never would be. But somewhere out there *was* the perfect bride for him. The one who would already know the diplomatic requirements of being a royal bride.

She watched their interaction with curiosity. Although their conversation seemed light, Mason could read the tension in Danyl's shoulders, and for a moment the soft, young features of the Princess slipped, and she saw an older, more compassionate woman replace the impression of a silly young girl. She nodded once, and placed her hand on Danyl's arm as if to convey understanding, and then in a second the mask was donned once more and she all but skipped off back to the other party guests. Confusion marked Mason's brow, one that jolted from shock when Danyl's unerring gaze found hers. And she saw the aide who had been waiting for them on the helipad approach Danyl, refusing to be cast aside this time.

Mason was finally free of the weight of Danyl's gaze. As she'd hoped, the aide had distracted him, taking his focus from her. She nearly let loose the ironic laugh. She'd always known that duty would distract him, but she never thought she'd be thankful for it.

The sun was beginning to dip behind the large sand-coloured, ornately decorated walls, the rays still desperately peeking out through the beautiful patterns in the stonework, falling onto the smooth-as-marble pool that lay like a sheet of amethyst in the hues of the setting sun. They had been away less than a day, less than seventeen hours even, but it had felt like years.

Whatever had passed between them, whatever they had done, Mason felt...differently at the palace now. She looked about, not seeing what could have been, or what had never been, but simply what was. A stunning piece of architecture and history, but it was so much more than that. It housed and protected the royal family. The country's rulers. And whilst many things had changed over the last few hours, that—for Danyl—had not. This palace, just like Danyl, was something to be proud of. He was a leader, a man to be proud of. She could see him ascending the throne, ruling his country with fairness, honesty, strength and compassion. She'd seen all those things in him now and even back then, ten years ago.

Many times she'd wondered what it would have been like, what would have happened, if she'd not pushed Danyl away. And always that imagined future had ended the same way. No matter what Danyl had said and thought, their love wouldn't have survived then. Not with the grief, the salacious news reports and media interest at the time. His reputation would have been tarnished by hers, the weight of duty and responsibility would have buckled their fragile young bonds. And in a way the last ten years had allowed them to grow up as people, as individuals, and Mason knew instinctively that it was right. That they had both needed that time and those years to do what they had done, to allow those years to shape them into the people they had become.

But who they would go on to be? That was a different question. Danyl's future was clear, but what of hers? The dossier that Danyl had presented her with, the proof that it was Scott who had caused not just Rebel's accident, but more... Guilt flared in her chest. The truth would enable her to race again, not just for the Winners' Circle, but for other trainers too, especially after the Hanley Cup.

As she turned away from the guests, away from the

gathering in the gardens, she wandered the pathways around the palace buildings, and wasn't that surprised when she came upon the stables. Whether she'd known where they were, or just sensed it, it didn't matter. She always had, and would always, find her way to them... her constant. Her safety. There were some incredibly fine horses here, she realised, glancing sideways at the spacious stalls with names that decried some of the most expensive and exalted lineages she'd ever seen in one place. But she only had thought of one.

A smile pulled at the corner of her mouth as Veranchetti's head bobbed through the opening of the stall door. Her hands reached up to his neck and she leant her forehead to his.

'Hello, V. It's been too long,' she gently whispered, for his ears only.

It was then that Mason realised she wouldn't be racing again. Her involvement in the Hanley Cup had only ever been about saving her father's farm. Sheer desperation and determination had seen her to the end of those three races. Not the joy or love of racing. And before that? An ache stirred in her breast as she acknowledged that it had only ever been a way to make her father proud. To somehow repay him for sticking with her after her mother had left. To justify the way he had sacrificed all his dreams to raise her.

It had been a long while since she'd thought of her mother. She had pressed that hurt as far down as she could beneath, yet somehow mixed with, her grief over Faaris and Danyl. It struck her then that she had done to Danyl what her mother had done to her. She had abandoned him when he'd needed her most, when *she'd* needed him most.

Guilt cracked against her like a whip, sudden, shocking and devastating. Veranchetti yanked his head back as if he'd felt it too, pulling out of her hold, leaving her hand free to rise to her mouth in horror.

Danyl cursed as he flew down the steps into the palace building. Where was she? The aide had given him the Prime Minister's latest white paper and had demanded to meet with him as soon as possible. But for once, Danyl couldn't jump to the tune of duty. He had to find Mason.

He ignored the curious glances of various dignitaries and guests who had remained at the palace following the gala. As he rounded the corner he almost walked straight into Dimitri and Antonio.

'There you are,' Antonio said, halting his progress.

'We wondered where you had got to,' Dimitri added.

'I had…business to attend to,' Danyl ground out, wondering why they didn't just move out of his way. He had to find Mason.

'That business have a name beginning with M?' Antonio taunted.

He pulled up short, finally greeting the knowing looks pasted across his friends' faces.

He nodded, almost incapable of words.

'Pay up,' Dimitri demanded of Antonio.

Danyl practically growled as Antonio handed over what looked to be at least one hundred dollars.

'You made a bet on me?'

'Only on the when, not on the who,' Antonio reassured him.

'Antonio thought it would take you a little longer. He had it down as Christmas Eve.'

'A little longer for what?'

'To come to your senses. Amata is nice enough...albeit a little young perhaps.'

'But you need someone like Mason. If she can handle Veranchetti, then she can handle—'

'I am not a horse,' Danyl rasped, barely able to keep the volume of his voice civil.

The amused looks grew serious.

'We know,' Antonio assured him. 'Just...take it easy, okay? She's clearly been through the wringer.'

He couldn't fault his friends for wanting to protect Mason, even at his own expense. Their bond was strong enough for that.

'I think she's at the stables,' Dimitri said, nodding head in the direction Danyl needed to take.

He found her beside the stalls, her hand at her mouth as if she'd been shocked by something. He thought then that he knew how she felt. The realisation of just how much he loved her had struck him hard and deep. He wanted to drag her to him, to tell her it would all be okay. But he just couldn't quite be sure of that yet. He was sure of himself, that he knew to be true. But looking at Mason here, in the stables, once again he was reminded of a wild horse, one that he feared might never be tamed.

She started when she noticed him, shifting from the shadows into the last beam of a setting sun. Dust particles shivered in the wake of her movements, looking like dull sparks and reminding him of the crystals on her dress from only hours before. As if she had morphed from the glittering, beautiful Princess of the night into the soot-covered Cinderella of the day.

'Danyl, I...'

'You saw me talking to Amata.'

She bit her lip, no soft seduction, no action drawn from arousal but from concern and worry. She nodded quickly.

'I was telling her that I was no longer able to entertain—'

'You shouldn't have done that.'

Danyl tempered the streak of anger igniting in his chest. He knew she'd struggle against this, against their feelings. Instead he sought the same control he used with any hurt, scared animal.

'If I am to be honest with myself, I owed it to Amata to be honest with her. I am done looking for a biddable bride, because...' he pushed on despite the fact her hand had come up between them as if in an attempt to ward off his words, his love '...because I know of a woman who is not biddable. Who is stubborn and determined and powerful and absolutely the only person I want to spend the rest of my life with.'

It hurt to see her shaking her head. But he pushed that away too.

'Danyl, you were right. We did need to confront the past, resolve our issues, address the past. But only so we could move on. Move on so that you could find a bride that would be a suitable queen.'

'If you believe that there is someone else out there more suitable for me, then you haven't understood anything in the last twenty-four hours.'

Mason sucked down the hurt of his accusation. Because those hours had meant so much to her, and given so much to her. She had felt healed by the sharing of the past, of the grief for their son, and of their exquisite passion. It had set her on a new path, one where she felt finally able to move ahead on the shaky legs of a newborn fowl. But for a moment that glimpse of hurt when she had woken up alone, when she had thought him closing down a future between them before coming back to Aram—that had shattered her heart into a thousand pieces. It was a thousand reflections of the loss and pain she'd always thought she'd feel when he finally tired of her. And instead of feeling hope when she saw him with Amata, instead of being soothed now by his words, she wanted them to stop. She wanted him to take them back. Because even just the reflection of his rejection was enough to create a panic in her chest like she'd never felt before. It was threatening her now. Tickling at the edges of her senses, closing up her throat and sitting on her chest. She knew it was fear. But its hold was strong.

'Have you? Understood what the last day has meant?' he demanded, his voice beginning to fray.

'Perhaps it just meant something different to me, Danyl.' She hated the pleading tone in her voice, but she desperately wanted him to understand. Understand that it was impossible. That she'd never believed in fairy tales where the Princess was swept off her feet and into the castle by the handsome Prince. That reality was mundane and difficult and painful, and even that was more bearable than having the fantasy ripped away.

'I told you. I told you how much it hurt when you pushed me away last time.' His words called to her, guilt mixed with fear making it all so much worse. He reached out and his thumb snagged her chin, bringing her to meet his gaze. The sincerity in his eyes, the pain, the love…it was all there for her to see.

'Don't do this again. Please don't do it again. I love you,' he whispered.

'I can't, Danyl. Please let me go.'

'No. Tell me. Tell me what you're running from again. Tell me what it is that you're afraid of.'

His accusation hurt and set fire to the cocktail of emotions coursing through her body. Flames of anger, hurt and grief licked her skin, burning and scorching. Because she was afraid of how she felt. She was afraid of her love for him. Because she *did* love him. She always had. And she knew in that moment that she always would.

'That you'll leave me just like my mother did!' she cried out, unaware of the unsettled horses stamping on the floor, picking up on her emotions.

'I am not your mother,' he said, his voice quiet and painfully reasonable in direct contrast to her own hysteria.

'We've spent a total of about twenty-five hours together.'

'Ten years ago we spent a hell of a lot more time together than that,' he growled.

'And in ten years people change! How can you think you're in love with me? How can you trust that?'

'How can you not trust yourself, Mason? How can you not feel it too? Or is it rather that you don't trust me enough to love you?'

And that was it. He could see it in her face, in her eyes, the way her body recoiled from his touch.

'Love is a leap of faith, Mason. Faith and trust in someone else. It never really mattered, did it? Whatever I did, it wouldn't have ever been enough.'

The moment the words had left his lips, he knew them to be true. He turned and walked away from the stables, away from Mason, away from the last piece of hope his heart had held.

CHAPTER TWELVE

December, present day

DANYL CLUTCHED THE glass of whisky in a death grip. He didn't know whether he wanted to hurl it across his office or crush it between his fingers. She had gone again. Despite all that they had shared in the last day, despite everything that had passed between them...despite his love for her...she had still left.

'You should probably put that glass down before you hurt yourself.'

'And you should probably both stop hovering in palace doorways,' Danyl said to Antonio and Dimitri.

He watched as they gingerly stepped over the threshold into his office.

'Really? It's my turn now?' he asked, seeing their faces grim with determination. 'Antonio, you got coffee... Dimitri, whisky. What do I get?'

'Me.' His mother's voice cut into the dark swirl of emotions surrounding him.

'Thank you, gentlemen,' she said, nodding to Antonio and Dimitri.

'Your Majesty,' they murmured in unison as Eliza-

beth bestowed upon them a beautiful smile, and they retreated from the room.

Danyl was too angry to roll his eyes.

'You shouldn't flirt with them. They're married men,
or as good as.'

'I don't know what you are talking about,' his mother
said lightly, her tone serving only to aggravate him
more.

He put the glass of whisky down, leaving a golden
ring on the Prime Minister's white paper.

'She has gone?'

'Yes, she has. Again.' His mother opened her mouth to
say something, but he pushed on, not wanting either questions or hypothetical explanations. 'Mother, I don't have
time for this. I need to meet with the Prime Minister.'

'I think that can wait.'

'Don't be silly. I won't make the Prime Minister wait.'

'Don't call me silly.' An icy edge had entered his mother's tone. The one that always made him sit up and listen. 'I am not just your mother. I am the Queen, and I
have been doing this a lot longer than you, Danyl Nejem
Al Arain. Of course you can make him wait. There are
some things more important, and there are some things
that *can* wait.'

In spite of all that Danyl felt, a streak of pride cut
through him as he saw his mother as the regal, powerful woman she was.

'Perhaps it's been a while since I saw you as Queen
and not just my mother,' he said, allowing a small, sad
smile to pull at the edges of his mouth.

'Perhaps it's been a while since you let me be Queen
and not just your mother,' she said, gesturing for him to
take a seat as if this were her office and not his.

He chose to ignore the fact that with him seated, and her perched on the edge of his table, he felt once again like a small child.

'I want to talk about when you came back from America.'

An ache opened up in his chest, and he was surprised to feel it keenly after all the pains of the last few hours. 'Not now,' he ground out.

'I think now is absolutely the right time, after all these years. I kept my silence back then, and perhaps I shouldn't have. When you came back from the States, you were not the same boy who had left. You weren't just changed by age, but by experience.'

'A lot happened there.'

'I know,' she said quietly, solemnly.

'I don't think you do.'

'I *do* know, Danyl. You're my son. I am neither blind, nor stupid. And neither are the staff we paid to take care of you and watch over you.'

Shock rippled through Danyl, and as he looked into his mother's eyes he saw compassion, understanding and grief. 'I am so sorry about what happened to you. I'm so sorry about what happened to you both. I can't...' she said, her eyes bright with the sheen of tears. 'I can't begin to understand it. I can imagine... I know what the fear of it feels like. But to lose a child, even so early on—'

Danyl put up a hand to ward off her words, just as Mason had done to him. The sympathy, the simple comfort that his mother was ready to offer... It was almost too much.

'It must have been devastating for you both. And I'd never take that away from you, I'd never ask you to cover that, or hide it. But what I want—as selfish as it is—is for my son to laugh, to smile and to love. I want to see those things again, the ones I heard through the phone and on Skype before such tragedy stole those abilities, those feelings, that happiness from my child.'

'I love her.'

'I know.'

'And she left. Again.'

'Why?'

'Because she fears that I will leave her like her mother did.'

Elizabeth seemed to take this in. Her sigh was just as heavy with the feelings that were crying out in his own chest.

'Did she say she didn't love you?'

He paused, for the first time since confronting Mason in the stables. 'No.'

'And you allowed her to leave.'

Danyl cursed, out loud. 'I can't keep her here against her will, Mother.'

'Then perhaps she was right to walk away.'

'How can you say that?' he demanded, his voice full of a pain he could no longer hide.

'Danyl, I love you. But when she left you, it took you ten years to put your faith back together. Put your love back together. She was a child when her mother left. What would that have done to her? How long would it take to recover from that?'

The question stalled him, robbed him of breath and thought. His mind careening from one fact to another, but snagging on what seemed like the most unimportant one.

'How did you know she was a child when her mother left?'

'I know a lot of things, Danyl.'

'Clearly.'

'Mason McAulty is a woman who has led a very different life from ours.'

'I know. Aussie outback—'

'That's not what I'm talking of. How old was she when her mother left?'

'She was two.'

'And her father?'

Danyl smiled at the memory of the bluff, hard man who had sent him to his daughter without a tent, on the back of a horse he slapped for good measure.

'Good. Honest.'

'Loving?'

'Yes, in his own way.'

'A way that is perhaps not so much about talking, and more about showing?'

He looked at his mother. Tried to read between the lines, tried to come to the conclusion she was leading him to.

And finally the question he asked himself… How had he shown her that he loved her? He had expected her to undo a lifetime of hurt in a day. He had expected her to jump at his declaration of love, but when it came down to it he had not shown her that he would stay with her. He hadn't stayed. He had allowed her to push him away, rather than fight with her, fight *for* her. Both then and now. Crashing waves of shock beat against his heart. All this time he had blamed her for leaving him, yet in reality he had let her go. He may have fooled himself into thinking that it was what she wanted, but he knew… now he *knew* that it had been easier for him to let her leave. Images of what might have been—had he argued with her, had he proved to her that he loved her, had he stayed and confronted both their fears—ran through his mind like a movie. It would have been painful, but they would have got through it. Together. All this time… Guilt and pain warred within his chest. For all his words of confronting his grief—honouring it—the one thing he hadn't honoured, *really* honoured, was his duty to her… his love for her.

'I have to leave.'

'And what about the Prime Minister?' his mother asked, with the largest smile he'd ever seen.

'He can wait.'

It had only been when she'd packed the last of the few things she'd come to Ter'harn with that Mason had re-alised she wasn't even sure how to get home. But it seemed that Danyl had thought of her even in her leaving of him. Michaels had knocked on her door, informed her that he would be taking her to the airport and booked her on a first-class flight back to Sydney with transfers back home. He'd swept her up with efficiency and dis-cretion, not ignoring her tear-stained appearance, but not acknowledging it either.

That was how she found herself sitting in yet another lap of luxury she was sure she couldn't appreciate, try-ing so very hard not to break down and cry. Her entire body ached from tension, exhaustion and just plain old hurt. He had told her he loved her. And she had left. He had asked her to take a leap of faith, and she hadn't been able to. And she hated herself for it. Hated that she was so locked in a cycle of fear, hated her mother for leaving such a legacy. She was so very sorry for the small child she had been, and still was in some ways, that was just scared of opening herself up to the possibility of happiness, of love, because if it was taken away again…she just didn't think that she'd survive.

Mason turned away from the air stewardess, who placed a glass of champagne and one of orange juice on the side table, clearly wary of intruding. Mason closed her eyes, pressed her head back against the seat and wished the plane would just take off.

There had only ever been Danyl. No one before, and no one since. She had been cruel when she'd told him that their relationship was candy floss, knowing that above all experiences in her life that was the one that really held true. But to think of that time, of those feelings of love…what they had shared was a childish precursor to the way she felt for him now as a man. A man who cared so deeply for his country, a man who had forged bonds of friendship within the Winners' Circle, and who was so clearly beloved of his parents. A man who, unlike her, had respected his grief, allowed himself to feel it. A man who knew himself so acutely and so strongly he was able to put himself on the line before her, lay himself bare to her. And still she'd rejected him. Danyl was, and always would be, a man who felt duty so acutely. She hadn't wanted to be a burden to him then, and wouldn't dream of being a burden to him now. God knew she'd been a burden to people long enough.

Her heart ached and she clenched her hands to try to stop the tremors she knew would be there, but the tears falling down her cheeks betrayed her and she couldn't do a thing to stop them.

An announcement in Arabic stole the attention of the

passengers and their reaction was enough to tell her that there was something wrong. It had just begun in English, when the sounds of sirens coming from outside the plane began to filter through the cabin.

She looked out to see four black, diplomatic estates being escorted by police cars, lights flashing, turning in a wide curve onto the runway.

Shivers took over her body, and she turned to find the air stewardess approaching her. In quiet tones the woman asked her to follow her please. Her cheeks burned as passengers craned their necks to look at her, muttering between themselves.

'What's going on? Is everything okay?' Mason asked the air stewardess as she began to unbuckle her seatbelt.

'Everything's fine, ma'am, but if you could come with me...' She directed Mason to the cabin door, and Mason was surprised to see a set of stairs leading down from the doorway. At the bottom stood Danyl, alone, in a dark, fine woollen coat torn open by the wind. A beautiful crisp blue shirt was flattened against taut stomach muscles and open at the neck.

'Danyl, what are you doing here? You're going to cause a scene.' Mason had still not taken a step down yet, calling to him, instead, from the doorway.

'I don't care.'

'But... I... I left.'

'No, I don't think you left. I think I let you go.'

'What?' She was confused, not quite sure where this was going, and not particularly enamoured of the fact that there was a whole planeload of people watching them.

'You didn't leave me. I just didn't stay with you.'

Mason's heart began to pound.

'Do you love me?'

Mason knew that she couldn't lie to him. He'd not asked before, but now he had…she just couldn't do it, because she did. She loved him so much.

From where he stood on the tarmac, he could see the truth she wouldn't yet speak. It was in her eyes, on her face and written across her skin. He allowed it to fill him, allowed it to give him the confidence he really did need at that moment.

'Well, I refuse,' he said, adopting the most arrogant tone he could, because he knew it would make her smile, he hoped it would make her laugh as she once had. As he once had.

'Refuse to what?'

'Leave you,' he said, taking one step up the stairs. 'Or allow you to leave me.'

'Because you're a prince?' she asked, her voice trembling.

'No, not because I'm a prince. But because I love you,' he said, taking another step up towards her. 'So I don't accept your decision to leave. And I won't allow you to let me go. Because I don't want to be let go,' he said, stepping upwards. 'I'm here to prove that I love you. Not because of the past, not because of a sense of duty, but because you make me laugh even in the midst of my sorrow, you make me hope even in my despair, and love even in my anger. I loved you then and I love you now, and no matter what you decide, choose or feel, nothing will take that away. You made and continue to make me into the man I am, standing here today, telling you that I love you. Hoping that you'll wear my ring, be my wife and partner, lover and teacher, and the mother of as many children as we can have.'

* * *

There was no stopping the tears now. Mason felt them falling down her cheeks, hurtling towards the ground so very far below her. With every single word he had undone her. He had slipped beneath the bonds that wrapped around her heart, holding it still. But now it was beating, hard and fast and completely for him. He had come back for her. He had refused to allow her to push him away. Refused to allow her to hide from her own feelings, and in doing so given her the strength she needed, to reach for the one thing she had always wanted. He had stopped midway up the stairs, and with shaking legs she took her first step towards him.

'Oh, Danyl, I love you too,' she said almost helplessly. 'Because no matter what I've done, how many times I've run from you, you've always seen to the heart of me. Even when no one else has, you've seen the truth and loved me for it—or in spite of it.' She took one more step closer to him. 'Because you've taken every demand I could possibly make and met it. You've always given me what I needed even when I couldn't see it for myself.' She stood one step above him, desperate to reach out to him, to hold him to her. 'I am known by you and am greater for it, and perhaps because of what we've shared, love and grief, our love will be stronger for it.'

'The past hasn't been and never will be forgotten, Mason. It is the fabric and the strength of our love. And I will spend each and every day proving that to you, if you will let me.'

Mason's answer was the most exquisite kiss Danyl had ever had. It was the sweetest, most powerful kiss, binding them together in a way that meant no future obstacle, no past hurt, would ever tear them apart. It was a kiss that defined what it was to love and be loved, and one they shared every day for the rest of their lives.

EPILOGUE

Christmas Eve, ten years later...

MASON BREATHED IN the scents of mint, eucalyptus and honey that rose from Faaris's garden in the Summer Palace. Over the past ten years, she and Danyl had spent so much time here that the garden was no longer locked. Instead, as their family had grown with the birth of their daughter, and later with their second son—because Faaris would always be their first—all four of them would come here to remember. More and more the sound of laughter rather than tears would filter through the beautiful gardens, and the hurts of the past had become not less...but something different. A part of the fabric of their lives, their loves and their hearts.

'I thought I would find you here.' Her husband's voice reached her from over her shoulder. He pulled her towards his strong body as they shared a moment, looking up at the fine statue of the knight. Mason smiled into the crook of his arm as she inhaled the scent of the man she loved so much she could not find the words.

'The children—'

'Are over-excited about the arrival of Dimitri and Antonio and their families. Honestly, I thought *we* were an entourage—but them?'

'Well, we can't exactly ask them to leave their families behind at Christmas, husband.'

'I wouldn't dream of it, wife.'

Mason looked up at Danyl then, seeing him as she had first seen him in the grand room at the Langsford and then, ten years later, in the darkness with a... She huffed out a laugh.

'What?'

'I still can't believe I pointed a shotgun at you.'

'I can.' He smiled, rubbing the base of her spine with his warm hand. 'You're as fearless now as you were then.'

Fearless. She wasn't sure that was how she would have described her feelings when Danyl had first taken the throne, during the hours she had spent learning the palace etiquette required of the Queen of Ter'harn. But she'd had an amazing support network. Danyl had been her rock. His mother, Elizabeth, had been kind and patient, and even Danyl's father had been generous and loving.

When the international press had uncovered Mason's mother's whereabouts there had definitely been some difficult moments, but she couldn't regret the relationship they now had. It wasn't always an easy one, and she had struggled with the guilt and hurt the burgeoning relationship had ignited within her. But both her father and Danyl had been there every step of the way. Her father had found love with Mary—the woman Danyl had arranged to help manage the farmstead in Australia in Mason's absence—and she couldn't imagine him with anyone else now.

With Emma Arcuri's help they had developed the

programme that helped children and teens interact with the horses to an international level, each member of the Winners' Circle hosting different locations around the world for a similar programme, all under the banner of the McAulty name.

She touched the necklace that Anna Kyriakou had designed. It was matched only by the one worn by her husband, designed in the image of a knight. Anna had presented them shortly after Mason had realised that she was pregnant. She marvelled at how close she, Emma and Anna had become. Perhaps as close as Dimitri, Danyl and Antonio themselves.

She smiled at the joy and peace that had come to her life, the contentment and the rightness of it all, and thought that maybe the fairy tales had it right. The handsome Prince *had* come and whisked her away to his palace to live happily ever after.

Danyl felt his wife shift beneath his arms, turning so that she could see him. His heart beat loudly and proudly in his chest for the amazing woman he felt he'd loved for his entire adult life, long before he'd ascended to the throne, all the way back to when he'd been a young man, doubtful of his future, worried about what kind of ruler he would be.

Even now he remembered the words she'd once said to him. He'd struggled sometimes not to let fear overwhelm him, but with Mason by his side he *had* made his own decisions, to the best of his ability. And he had become a ruler that his people believed in and loved. But, he reflected, his greatest achievement was most definitely persuading this incredible woman to become his wife, mother to his children, and Queen of his country.

After one final and most definitely passionate kiss,

Danyl led her back to the Summer Palace, where it had become their Christmas tradition to greet the rather large brood of friends and family gathered over the years.

Antonio and Emma Arcuri were there, as were their mothers and Antonio's sister—always on hand to help them with their three children. Dimitri and Anna arrived shortly after, with their two children. Anna's parents came, each with their respective spouses, and Dimitri's stepmother. Joe McAulty and Mary, his wife, were already busying themselves around the kitchen, the staff having finally got used to Mary's affectionate determination to 'help out' with Christmas dinner. Joe was also here somewhere—most likely at the stables, checking on Veranchetti—but he'd arrive just in time for the meal. His own mother and father had embraced 'retirement', as his mother called it, and were now glorying in spoiling all the children with enough sugar and presents to have each parent sincerely concerned about bedtime.

Christmas might not be part of Ter'harn's religious calendar, but it was a day when each and every one of them celebrated family, friendship and the bonds of love that had drawn them all together.

As Mason's fingers threaded through his Danyl felt those invisible bonds manifest, and brought her hand to his lips.

'I don't know what I would have done without you,' he whispered to his wife.

'You were never without me. I was always here,' she said, tapping his chest where his heartbeat responded to her touch. 'As you were with me. Always.'

* * * * *

LET'S TALK

Romance

For exclusive extracts, competitions
and special offers, find us online:

f facebook.com/millsandboon

⊙ @millsandboonuk

🐦 @millsandboon

Or get in touch on 0844 844 1351*

For all the latest titles coming soon,
visit millsandboon.co.uk/nextmonth